Stealing Away

stories

KEVIN REVOLINSKI

BACK BURNER BOOKS
MADISON, WISCONSIN

Back Burner Books
17 Sherman Terrace #4
Madison, WI, 53704
www.BackBurnerBooks.net

This book is a work of fiction. The characters, incidents, and
conversations are entirely created by the author. Any resemblance to actual
events or persons, living or dead, is entirely coincidental, and in no way
intended by the author.

Four of the stories included in this collection have appeared in other
publications in slightly different forms:
"La Gatita" in *The Summerset Review*, "Mosaic" in *Red Wheelbarrow
Literary Review*, "On a Raft in Green Water" in *South Dakota Review*, and
"Thirst" in *Westview*

Cover photos by Preamtip Satasuk
Author photo by James Clark
Cover design by Back Burner Books

Library of Congress Control Number: 2020925486

ISBN: 978-1-7363341-0-2 (Paperback)
ISBN: 978-1-7363341-2-6 (ebook)

First Edition: January 2021

For Grandma G., my first storyteller

Table of Contents

Stealing Away

Stealing Away

"LEAVE IT IN neutral. When I nod, just pull your foot off the brake. It'll roll. So watch until the back tires hit the street, then crank hard right. Got it?"

"Sure," I said, trying to sound bored though my palms were sweating, my heart pushed up into my throat, and I thought I might freaking wet myself.

"And don't forget to straighten the wheels once you're in the street or you'll put it in the ditch."

"No, really?" For a moment indignation overlaid fear.

"Jesus, Diane, why are you always so sarcastic?" Danny gave me that disappointed look which disappeared under my eye roll. He had unscrewed the dome light at the beginning of the trip, so it remained dark as he got out of the car and closed the door gently as if he were laying a baby in a crib. Even so the click startled me like a gunshot. When he hunched over the hood and nodded, I let out the brake. The incline of the driveway did all the work so he barely needed to push. The car bounced a bit as it passed over the sidewalk, and I started turning the wheel and eased back onto the brake. He came running with his arms waving, so I stopped completely.

"What the hell are you doing?" he hissed, as heartfelt as a shout, but not loud enough to reach any of the dark windows of the houses on either side of the street.

I shrugged, and he got in, slumped into the seat without fully closing the door. "You could have let it roll halfway to the neighbor's, give us a little distance."

"Doesn't matter."

"You better hope not. Want me to start it?"

I ignored the question and turned the key, letting out my breath when the car started on the first try. I put it in drive and it rolled forward on the idle until we reached the stop sign at the end of the block. Then I turned on the headlights and headed back out toward the highway. I was officially a felon.

Grand larceny. I had looked it up. Anything stolen worth more than five hundred dollars. Assuming this junk heap was worth five – which I doubted, though an idiot had just paid us six – this was a Class 3 felony. In Illinois, anyway; I hadn't checked Iowa. That's two to five years and up to twenty-five grand for a fine. My entire world, including my mother and everything she had, wasn't worth twenty-five K.

Danny insisted I pull over so he could drive. Back on the interstate we had all the windows rolled down, and he let out a war whoop, banging his hand on the outside of the door as we

4

raced off into the night, the wind whipping our hair around. Bonnie and Clyde. It took us another hour driving around in the dark until we found a place south of a wildlife refuge that had looked pretty good on Google Earth: a two-tire dirt path off a county highway ran the border between woods and cornfields. We drove in far enough that we couldn't see the occasional passing cars out on the road behind us. Danny pitched the tent, unrolled the bag, and we lay there several moments without speaking, listening to the buzzing and chirps of a million insects, the rustle of cornstalks in the gentle breeze, and the unnerving hum of channeled lightning running above us in high-tension wires.

"Aren't those sort of dangerous? Stray voltage, brain tumors or whatever?"

Danny snorted. "Maybe if you live by them for ten years. We're fine."

Danny's sleeping bag had a scratchy lining with a pattern like a kilt. The zipper had broken the first night, so we laid it out like a blanket and rolled ourselves into it like a human double taco. We had picked it up at Wal-Mart, hanging our heads like they do in liquor store robberies in hopes that the security cameras didn't I.D. us – if someone eventually bothered to try to track us down. Soon Danny was snoring lightly, while I lay awake trying to see stars through the screen material in the dome of the tent. The strong scent of pine drifted in on the breeze reminding me of my mother's favorite evening refreshments.

NANCY WAS A food-stamp mom, and it was crazy how everyone seemed to know that. Kids keep score and share intel. She at least

5

bothered to go down the highway a bit and shop at a grocery store where we'd likely not see anyone we knew. But still, she stood there at the checkout, watching the totals, looking down at the government-supplied debit card as if she might guess the balance by hefting it in her open palm.

I could have gotten free lunch at the high school – several of us could've, in fact – but no way, not with all those eyes and ears and the accompanying sharp mouths. High school is shitty enough with bullies who pick your flesh with whatever hook they can hang on you, from the size of your nose to the brand of your footwear. So food stamps? Mortifying. I started calling her by her first name when I was a sophomore. I know it pissed her off, but she took it in stride – which pissed me off. One for the win column for Nancy.

Danny had both parents, but they had the spirit of god running all through them and basically anything Danny said, did, or thought about doing was forbidden or punished. And with the supreme judge being silent, invisible, and all, there really wasn't room for appeals. If his parents had known what we did out behind the equipment shed at the end of the football field some afternoons, he'd be grounded for life or cast in fires or both. Nancy would slap down another lame curfew and lecture me about the dangers of reproduction. It didn't take a genius to know I was one of her consequences.

As required, Danny spent Sunday mornings at "worship" which had become a noun apparently. The Church of Eternal Life, a pole barn north of town with a big sign outside that read "Faith Free." I suggested we ought to hyphenate that so like there's this place where those of us still pretty doubtful

6

about the whole thing might get together. Danny either didn't find it funny or didn't get it, but he nodded vaguely, distracted by something else. He fought with his parents a lot, volleying throat-tearing streams of obscenities at them while I waited in his tired, last-century Chevy Cavalier in the drive. He'd come out with the face of a cherub, as if he had just kissed them goodnight, a hand swoop putting his long bangs back in place. I was never sure which performance was real, the indoor or the outdoor one. He always seemed to get his way, however. "Everything is negotiable," he said, with that grin that only lifted the right side of his smile.

It was the summer before senior year when Danny and I decided the adults in our lives had irredeemably failed us, and so we hit the road. The plan was to live by hunting and gathering. We'd had practice for a couple years, often wandering through the aisles of the minimart across from school, scanning the shelves for attractive snacks that fit the palm and then the pocket. A pasty girl, Judy, with big glasses and vaguely defined body lines, worked the counter. I think she thought I was one of the cool kids. A recent dropout, she definitely wasn't – neither was I, to be honest – but if she wanted to earn brownie points and kiss up to a high school student, that was fine. She'd smile, glossless lips pressed together to keep the rack of braces inside. And then if she saw me next to, say, the donuts, she'd look away suddenly, turn her back and pretend to be occupied with something. I could put an entire donut in my mouth in one go. Blink and you'd miss it but for the reddening face as I held my breath while trying to tongue-mash it into something I could swallow. The benefits of a round face and chipmunk-fat cheeks. Adorable, Nancy used to say, but adorable is a social death sentence by the end of fifth grade. Danny came up with the idea: sell his car on Craigslist – repeatedly. He'd set up a fake email account and dangle the bait in a different town each time. Hand over a fake title for cash, come back that night with a second set of keys and drive off. We'd aim west toward Portland, Seattle, maybe northern California. We hadn't decided, because it didn't matter. Far away was good enough. Danny stole a license plate off the front of a car over in Rockford, and then swiped an annual registration sticker, which, though made to tear if you pulled it off, could easily be peeled away intact if the owner had several years stacked on top of each other on the plate – which is like always.

DANNY AND I woke up to the pre-dawn light with the lumps of the earth in our backs. I leaned into his back and breathed him in, still nervous and excited that we had actually done it, left it all behind. We'd face it all together. I closed my eyes for a bit more and was drifting away again when Danny's sniffing brought me back. "You smell that?"

"Skunk?"

"Jesus."

Our eyes watered as Nature's own horrible tear gas drifted through our campsite. We gathered our stuff as if we were escaping a burning building and shoved it all in the trunk in a rustling ball. The car rattled back along the dusty trail, then bounced up onto the pavement with a bark of the tires as we continued west. He already had someone interested another two hours away.

Danny's cell company was cheap and local so as soon as we had crossed the Mississippi he lost coverage for his iPhone. "Doesn't matter. We can't use it for this anyway. Traceable," he said. We picked up a TracFone at Wal-Mart and rationed the minutes, business only. Not having a cell phone myself was almost as mortifying as food stamps, but my mother insisted that it'd make me resourceful. "I never needed one growing up so why should you?" But I knew the truth was she couldn't afford the extra bill, and yet she wouldn't let me work, insisting, "Now is the one time you can be free from a job, and besides, it affects your studies. Foolish kids get a taste for a pathetic little paycheck and then they figure to buy a truck and drop out to work more to pay for it."

"You think I want a *truck*? Thanks, *Nancy*."

"Well, no, not you, *Diane*. But you know what I mean." I wasn't always the one she was angry at, but I received all the messages.

Danny and I stopped at a public library and he got on the internet to check Google maps for the next cities down the highway. He placed a couple more Craigslist ads and checked his inbox. "Hey, got another one!" His voice came loud and he brought it down to a whisper as he made sure none of the heads bent around us looked up. "No, two! Shit, maybe we can sell it twice in one day."

"Are they in the same town?"

"No. About an hour apart." He tapped his finger on the computer monitor, some dirt visible under his nail.

That seemed like a risk somehow, or maybe a complication, juggling two appointments. "That sucks."

He gave me that look that said I was stupid. "Or it doesn't. Too risky to pull this off twice in one town. Think about it." Because unless someone tells me to think, I don't, apparently. I hid the eye roll by pausing to look at the big round clock above us.

Danny slid his "fancy paper" into the printer and made an additional deed and dropped a quarter at the checkout counter on our way out. He kept it in a folder that still said "Chem" on it. I admired that he never threw anything away.

WHEN WE LEFT my father in Chicago, Nancy and I just bolted. Rather than facing him about it, she left a note. They had never married, so there really wasn't much he could say about it, plus even as a pre-schooler I could sense we were barely tolerated house guests. They didn't even fight. Nancy would ask questions, receive no answers, then ramp it up a notch until she was screaming so loud – about money, groceries, responsibilities, needs – that I would cover my ears in the next room and slip into the space behind the couch where I'd lie on my back. He battled her with silence and cigarette smoke.

Nancy and I headed west from Chicagoland to Rockford when I was five, one of the top ten worst places to live according to a website, and I remember her driving us around the streets and me helping load things into the trunk from the curb for our new place. "Scavenger hunt" she called it. "OK, now we need to find a lamp. Maybe if we're lucky an old TV." Over the years as she made bits of money, she replaced most of the items, the old toaster, a box fan for the window, an easy chair that smelled like old people. But we still kept a glass-topped coffee table, a memorial to those foraging years. I used to sit on the living room carpet putting together puzzles she'd picked up from garage sales or the St Vincent de Paul Society. Scenes of seaside Italy or Greece, villas painted the bright colors of a baby's room or gleaming white in the sun. Nothing like rural Illinois, the shades of dust and dung, brittle gray in the long winters, pale wilting green in the hot summer. The jigsaw villas cast their colors in the water, and a lone sailboat, empty and waiting, moored just offshore. I put them together over and over, but not one of them came complete, a couple holes short of a vision of paradise.

Predictably, Rockford didn't last. Nancy hated my first-grade teacher, Mrs. McClaskey, a sweater-wearing, church-society grandma type with Kleenex tucked into one sleeve for easy access. "She asks too many questions," she said, dragging me along half-off-balance as she stomped back to the car. My parent-teacher conference was less about math and reading and more of an investigation into whether there was a man in the house and what Nancy fed me for breakfast. The next summer we migrated west again, to Nelsonville, an even smaller town, though not on anyone's lists of anything good or bad. No place.

We rarely talked about my father over the years. Nancy said, "You win some, you lose some. The trick is to leave the table before you lose it all." She got out. "Cashed in the chips," she said. She worked at a casino as a cocktail waitress almost an hour's drive from Nelsonville, so her choice of words showed her lack of imagination. (I told her so once; she ignored me, blew a smoke ring at the kitchen light, cool as can be. So she had perhaps learned one thing from my father.) She took me to the casino only twice, to pick up a check or something, and I wandered around a bit, unsupervised. Unlike the glamorous appeal of Vegas in the movies or the uber-classy James Bond scenes, the shabbily-dressed gamblers hunched zombielike over chump-change slot machines. Like something from a sci-fi thriller, most of them were plugged into what looked like tiny scuba tanks feeding breath through a plastic tube to their noses, keeping them alive where they lived underwater. They had to step outside to smoke – which they did, of course, with no sense of irony. At least something is more important than the game, I guess.

WE WAITED AT Danny's suggested meeting spot, in the lot in front of a strip-mall Radio Shack. A wiry guy in a dress shirt and jeans pulled up in a Toyota Corolla that looked nicer than Danny's Cavalier. He stepped out of the car like he had nowhere to go, so Danny called out: "Hey, are you Sam?"

The guy turned and looked back and forth between us. Danny lost his slouch and I was reminded how tall he really was.

"You're Bob?"

Danny had a fake ID he'd use in liquor stores in neighboring towns. His genetic talent for making facial hair as a teenager and the laminating skills of professional nerd Donnie Ripkowski never drew a suspicious look.

"Bob Wilson, yes. This is it. Wanna take her for a spin?"

We drove around for about ten minutes in awkward silence but for the occasional question Sam struggled to come up with. "Mostly city or highway miles?" Sam didn't have a clue. "Handles OK." He fidgeted with the fan, turned the radio on and off. When we pulled back into the parking lot he parked next to his Corolla. "You mind?" He reached under the dashboard to release the hood.

"Not at all, Sam."

Danny kept using the guy's name in every sentence. It seemed too damn contrived, and I wanted him to stop. Surely the guy might catch on. I mean, who talks like that? But Sam got out, big dumb smile on his face, felt around for the latch and lifted the hood so he could stare at the engine. We joined him, and I wondered what he could possibly learn just by looking. I suppose any gaping holes or unattached hoses or wires might mean something. He even pointed and mumbled as if going through a checklist in his head, but it reminded me of the priest back when mom dated a churchy fellow for two long months of Sundays. Sam blessed the engine with a vaguely wandering finger as he completed the manly ritual of pretending to check under the hood.

He let it drop with a bang, thrust his hands in his pockets, and forced a short sigh, twisted up his mouth. "How much did you say again?"

Danny didn't answer right away. We all stood motionless. Like a Mexican standoff. I had to stifle a nervous giggle. As if remembering his line finally, Danny said, "It's six hundred."

Sam sucked his teeth, which I wanted to slug.

"I dunno. Kind of a lot of miles. That rust spot goes all the way through." He pointed to the rear tire well, but Danny didn't turn to look. "Will you take five?"

Danny let it hang there for a couple beats. "I need six, Sam. Like I said in the post, we're leaving the area, heading to Florida to take care of my grandmother. Gonna need every penny we can round up, you know?"

I admired the *cojones* Danny had right then. *I need six, Sam.* So confident, in control.

Sam gritted his teeth, stared off across the road thinking, or pretending to. "I guess I'll pass."

Danny sucked his teeth just like Sam had, for effect. "Well, damn, Sam, you are a bargainer. I can go five-fifty, Sam."

Sam's hand shot out and Danny shook it. We followed Sam back to his house, a white split-level with green shutters, faded siding, and a trailer with a boat under a tarp parked off the drive on a dead patch of grass. He paid us in tens and twenties, and Danny pulled the title out of the glove compartment. He retrieved our backpacks and reassembled camping bag from the trunk and handed over the keys. With the sound off, Danny sneaked a photo of the house and its number on his signal-less iPhone before getting into Sam's back seat. As agreed, Sam took us to the bus station where we would wait for our fictional ride to meet us. It took us an hour to walk the three miles back to his house that evening. We slipped the backpacks into the back seat, rolled out of the driveway, and were back on the interstate in fifteen minutes. Easy peasy.

I THINK NANCY might have liked Danny if he weren't dating me. She had the occasional boyfriend over the years. Nothing worked out for more than a few months. A couple of nervous one-night shitbags freaked out when they sneaked past the kitchen in the morning and saw me drooped over my generic corn flakes. She came out sometime later, dressed for the day, smoothing her blouse. I never said anything at the moment, but I'd bring it up when we argued about grades, concerts I couldn't go to, or the fact I couldn't work or stay over at a friend's. I called them her sex toys. Her smoke ring attempts became harsh bursts like from a steam whistle, so maybe that actually got under her skin.

So did Danny. "He's overbearing." I'm not sure she ever liked any of my few friends; the only variance was in the degree of hate or tolerance. Paul, a homecoming date, was "boring, probably eats paste." Danny the First, as she eventually referred to him when I started seeing Danny the Second, was "a kiss ass and smarmy." Bridgette, my BFF freshman year, was "a stuck-up bitch." Bridgette got on the pompon squad the next year, and suddenly she was not best, friend, or forever. So maybe she got that one right.

Our fights always progressed the same way. Nancy would stare at me over the kitchen table, calmly laying out the limits, the judgments, and the rules. A cigarette in one hand, an iced glass of gin in the other. I'd accuse her of not trusting me – although now that I think about it, she left a giant green bottle of Tanqueray right there on top of the fridge and cigarettes smack in the middle of the table. I'd start screaming at her in gradually increasing distances – from across the table, from the kitchen door, from the living room, the bottom of the steps, the top, and then one final formless burst of rage, unable to coalesce into words before being punctuated by the slam of my bedroom door.

WE SOLD THE CAR again at the western end of Iowa. This time for five hundred to a nice old lady who wanted to give it to her grandson, who sounded like a douche.

"He's such a good kid. I don't see him too much because getting around can be so difficult for him, and he's always so busy with school so he doesn't get time to call or write even. My daughter – his mother – we don't really talk all that much. Not since a long time."

"This is a good starter car, ma'am."

I stood behind grandma and shook my head. Danny didn't look at me, but he saw me.

"I think he's going to love it."

She gave him five crisp hundred dollar bills. We drove it to her house and she gave us a lift back to the mall where we'd told her our mother would be picking us up to head back to Des Moines. She offered to take us all the way there, and we had to convince her there was no way to call off the ride: my mother had no cell phone, she was likely almost there, it was very sweet of her to offer.

We killed time in the food court until the mall closed at nine, then started walking. The breeze and a dip in temperatures brought an evening chill, and I pulled a light jacket from my pack. Danny didn't stop but walked slower, and so I ran to catch up.

"I like the old folks. Cash is king. Like the ink wasn't even dry on those." He waved his arms palms up, fingers splayed like claws with his pleasure.

"I feel kinda bad."

"Oh, stop. It's only five hundred. You saw her house. She's

just fine. And how lame is that, trying to bribe your kid with a car to come visit."

"Grandkid."

"Yeah, but also her daughter. She figures that grumbly bitch is going to have to thank her, too."

"I don't think so. At some point you give up on people. You could tell how she felt about the boy is way different from how she sort of waves off her daughter like 'What's the point?' sort of thing."

"Mind-reading, are you?"

"No, just paying attention."

"And I'm not? You sure know better."

I thrust my hands deeper into my jacket, drawing my arms tighter to myself against the chill, elbows locked. For a second I remembered Mom making me straighten and lock my arms so she could lift me straight up on my fists for fun. I must have been four or five. I pulled my hands back out and hugged myself. "It's just I've seen that before. The body language. The tone of voice. It's how my mom talked about my dad."

We walked in silence a bit before he found a new subject. "What should we get with it? Should we eat out?"

"I thought we were saving for rent."

"Live a little, Diane."

"Aren't we?"

We waited across the street, walking slowly up the block, turning around a couple blocks later, and repeating the route until the living room light went out around 10:30. "Watching the news," I said. A half hour later the light in the back window on the side of the house opposite the garage went out as well.

We waited another fifteen minutes before circling back and slipping quietly into the car with the spare keys. Danny put it in neutral, and the incline of the driveway let the car roll into the street. He had to pull hard on the wheel to turn it without the power steering. Cringing, he turned the ignition and we drove away with the lights off until we reached the end of the block.

DANNY AND I met sophomore year during my goth phase. I buzzed my hair super short on one side, dyed it all black, and left the bangs long enough that I could tilt my head forward and hide behind them. Mom caught her breath when she saw it. I know she loved my long hair, but it looked like crap to me, ugly. Who ever came up with the color "dishwater blonde?" What an awful way to describe someone's appearance. But she regained her balance, tossed the car keys onto the counter as she reached above the fridge, and took me in from half-shaved-for-brain-surgery head to Doc Martens and shrugged. "At least you're making clothes shopping easier for me."

Danny and I ate together with the little community at the funereal moping table in the cafeteria and found each other in the back row of history class at second semester. He was affectedly aloof, plus cute and funny, and I was nobody. Yet he took me seriously. He'd look me in the eye and then literally turn an ear to me, as if maybe he had bad hearing in the other one. I had someone's attention and not just Nancy or a guidance counselor hovering over my back telling me what I should be doing. Throughout our junior year we'd cut class on occasion and cross to the quickie mart where pasty Judy would sell cigarettes to us. We'd smoke them, sitting on the curb in front, shoulder to shoulder, sharing a fake cherry fruit pie held in its packaging. He'd let me lay my head on his shoulder, and I'd listen to his fantasies about getting out of school. Maybe move to the mountains, work a ski lift. When he started saying "we," I got a warm feeling in the bottom of my throat, though I figured most of the plans were only talk at that point.

I had to wonder if Judy, staring at the high school all day, waiting for us to break for smokes or snacks, ever regretted dropping out. Didn't matter, I guess. I don't think she could have ended up with much better in that town had she stuck it out, and I am sure she couldn't even imagine something better, which is the problem, really. Mr. Summerset, the teacher for AVID, the catchy name of what the rest of us called an at-risk program, wanted Nancy to put me in, telling her: "It's hard to sell someone on a better life or the point of college if they don't see any of that in the world they live in." That pissed her off. Anyway, Nancy had gone to college, so she said, and look where that got us. I dreaded the idea of the two-year pseudo college in No Place.

Nelsonville occupied the bottom rung of life's ladder. The lower class – no judgment here, I am one of them – had made like the Okies in that brick of a book we were supposed to read this past summer and headed west from Chicago to crap-holes like Rockford. When the spit shine – emphasis on the spit – wore off there, they kept going and rented in Nelsonville or even bought up a cheap house in the revolving door of foreclosure. Nelsonville, a scab on the map, coagulating out of a thin farming population and the Rockford rejects, all huddled around the short strip of Main

19

Street with its parade of failed businesses. Somehow we have our own high school, otherwise it'd be a half hour bus ride to Martinsville. Leaving didn't require much effort, and yet it did require a reason.

Nancy caught me reading the school-assigned Steinbeck book and gave me an appraising look, maybe impressed even. "When you are young and stupid, you go for whatever is exciting at the moment. You know why women buy those horrible books with the shirtless guy on them? Because it'll never happen to them. Who wants some depressing real-life drama when most of us have that at home already? Where's a ticket out?" She puffed out with disgust, and a bit of smoke escaped. "There's your ticket out," she said, pointing at the book with her cigarette. I wasn't sure what she meant. The story? School? Route 66, "the road of flight"?

Nancy had long black hair with a white streak in it off to the left and a few other random white-gray strands scattered throughout. It reminded me of a black and white photograph she had, a close-up of her sitting inside a tangle of driftwood that had been dumped up on the shore of Lake Superior. The curving lines of her hair, the line of her jaw, her angular nose, and then the parallel lines of dark and light etched deep in the wood so far removed from its previous life as a tree. Elegant if you looked at it in its new life as something cast off but dignified. The hair made me think of her as the Bride of Frankenstein, someone struck by lightning. I never said, but I secretly thought it was cool that, one, she didn't dye her hair to hide it, and two, it looked like how kids my age were dyeing theirs. We weren't buddies, but maybe we could be one day. She'd dump the dishes in the sink to leave them for their 48-hour resting period. "Let them soak," she'd say. "Easier to clean later."

A LIGHT RAIN forced us to roll up the windows, and the air in the car got humid and funky like wet shoes. Danny surfed the radio through several Jesus and country music stations until landing on classic rock. Steve Miller Band's "Take the Money and Run" came on two songs later and I smiled: Billy Joe and Bobbie Sue, young lovers on the run. I turned to Danny to see if he caught it, but he looked far ahead, watching for state troopers and checking his speed.

Mom loved the Steve Miller Band, but the songs all sounded the same to me. "This was standard issue in college. Everyone played this at parties." It all sounded a bit too peach fuzz and happy to me. Give me something loud to grind to. Nine Inch Nails. We all wanted to disappear into it. No one loses themselves in that milquetoast "Keep on Rockin' Me, Baby" stuff.

I confess, as she was losing me, I could see something sad in her face, that zigzagging vein like the Harry Potter scar, striking down from her hairline at her electric blue eyes. (Mine were brown. Like mud.) Her cool had fled her the last few months, and she raised her voice in step with mine. There was anger, sure, but it faltered like a fluorescent bulb flickering as it couldn't hold a light. I saw anxiety and fear in the darkness in between.

When I was maybe six or seven, she used to tease me when I was home alone, waiting for her to come back from work – she never used a sitter. She'd call through the windows or tap

21

at the back door and run to the front. One time, as I worked on a coffee-table puzzle in the living room, her disembodied head suddenly appeared in the darkened screen window right at eye level, and she shrieked like a banshee. I nearly pissed myself it scared me so bad. I blew up at her, told her I hated her, and curled up in my own arms in the corner of the couch, I was so mad. She came running inside, laughing even as she apologized and tried to hug me, but I wasn't having it. It was the after-emotion from being shit scared, the wake of fear spreading out through me. The fear of being alone there, of her not protecting me, of never seeing her again maybe. The anger comes from someplace like a twisted message. "I wouldn't be angry at you if I didn't care," she once said, grounding me for a week for coming home at two a.m. when I still had an eleven p.m. curfew. I didn't understand that connection or realize I could feel the same until much later. Hindsight is a lame consolation prize. You didn't win but here's a 10% off coupon at a store you don't shop at. Thanks for nothing.

I came home one night, and Nancy and her latest beau, Billy – red flag on any adult male who still goes by Billy – were schizoid on the couch. McDonald's packaging spread across the coffee table. Amid the ketchup smears and burger wrappings with those orphaned bits of plastic cheese with squared edges, Billy had laid out and arranged a long line of blow on the glass like a freshly planted row in our landlord's garden in the back yard. They had taken a drinking straw, striped yellow and red like the corporate clown, and cut it in half. I let the door swing open and they froze like raccoons in the center of the highway at night. Nancy began wiping her upper lip though there was nothing there. Billy stared at a random spot on the wall as if it were the TV five feet up and to the left. No one spoke. Not being an idiot, I assessed the situation with a glance at each face and the table. She moved to speak, but I shook my head. "Whatever." I plodded up the stairs to my room. Slam the door? Yes, I decided. Loud noises maybe would freak them out. I suddenly felt possessive of that coffee table. I remembered a sailboat moored in a marina in Portofino. Both of us were looking for an escape from that living room, I guess. I called Danny in tears, and he signed on to Craigslist while I sniffled on the end of the line. As Nancy once put it: "Security," she said. "It's hard to walk away from." But then maybe it isn't really security if you can.

I WOKE UP, disoriented, the hum of the engine and the tires on the highway, the roar of the wind hot and dry. Nothing of the terrain suggested we were any farther than where I had nodded off five minutes or two hours ago. Dry grasslands and cornfields, either flat-lined or with a lazy roll to it. What hope was there out here? What point? Towns as small as Nelsonville but without the reassurance of a nearby real city of some worth rising up above the earth rather than staining it apologetically.

We had sold the car four times now, and if we were careful we'd have enough for first and last month's rent somewhere. Somewhere cheap, anyway. But the next day, making our way out of Dikesville or Dickeyville, we drove a bit too fast over a speed bump leaving a county park where we had pitched the tent for the night. The car sounded angry about that.

"Shit." Danny slowed and pulled over, leaving the engine idling with a deep rumble as if it was coming down with a chest cold.

"What's wrong?"

"Muffler."

"So?"

"Think about it. Costs money to fix a muffler, Diane."

"I'm not stupid. So don't fix it."

He paused, considering a smart-ass remark, but passed. "We gotta fix it. Mufflers get you pulled over. And two teenagers in a car? Don't give them a reason."

"Now what?"

He rubbed his eyes, and pinched his nose, thinking a moment. "We keep going."

An hour outside of Omaha we stopped for gas. The McDonald's inside had free WiFi so he stood outside the window smoking a cigarette and checked his phone for emails. "Yo. Got an offer."

"What about the muffler?"

He squinted down the road like he was gauging the time by the position of the sun. "No time. Maybe find a Car-X or whatever they have around here. If I email this guy and he gets back to me fast, we might even be able to sell the car by the end of the day. Enough to pay for the muffler tomorrow."

"No way he's paying full price with it like that though."

Danny looked away, then shrugged. "It is what it is."

"And it ain't what it ain't," I said, walking away. "And what I is, is hungry." I went inside and ordered only a double cheeseburger off the Dollar Menu. Halfway back to the car, I reconsidered not ordering a drink and went back in to the convenience store side. A bell sounded like an idea when I opened the door, and I nodded at the acne-faced guy with the little red vest. No bulletproof glass in this part of the country, though I expected there were plenty of guns to go around.

I wandered down one aisle and up another, stuffed some Ho-Hos into my hoodie pockets, and then came around the end to fill a large fountain soda cup with diet Mountain Dew. "I did a paper on that shit. Aspartame. It'll give you brain tumors," Danny told me a couple hundred times. I know how he did research papers straight off of Facebook links, and he mispronounced it 'ass-PAR-ta-may.' I figured he wouldn't even notice anyway. I figured wrong. A mile down the highway, he rolled down his window and spit his first sip into the wind, the pee-yellow drips running parallel to the road along the back-seat window. "The fuck, Diane?!"

"Best wash that off before someone asks for another hundred-dollar discount."

"Yes, you best."

He didn't take his eyes off the road and wiped the back of his hand across his mouth like he had lipstick that wouldn't come off. Drama queen.

"I don't know how you can drink that shit."

"It's surprisingly easy, actually."

"I bet you are."

I held my tongue; such a lame and rude comeback didn't merit a return.

I moved the big cup to my side of the drink holder under the dash and handed him a napkin as a peace offering. "You can get your own, you know. No sense one of us being unhappy over a fucking soda."

HE DRESSED LIKE a Nebraska accountant, or how I imagined one, I suppose. He climbed down out of a big pickup truck, buttoned up collared shirt, pants they would call "slacks" at JC Penney, formal cowboy boots. But his build made him look uncomfortable, too big for a desk job. Dark hair along the backs of his hands disappeared under his cuffs. He wore a mullet waiting to happen; give it a couple more weeks for the party in back to grow and trim the business in front. The mustache needed maintenance unless he meant to look like a '70s porn star. In fact, I have no idea what made me think accountant. Something exact and careful about him. He didn't know what to do with his hands, so they rose from his hips with vague gestures but never came higher than where his ribs must be, like a cowboy in a Western poised and ready to draw from both holsters.

He looked us over as much as the car and when he spoke to Danny his gaze slipped over to me, even for questions. "Any major repairs? Head gasket or the like?" I caught myself shrugging as Danny answered, and the guy nodded at me, "Uh-huh. Uh-huh. Decent mileage?" I pretended to see something interesting off to the left in the distance, but when I turned back he was still looking at me as Danny bullshat him about "20-something in town, but 30-plus on the highway, 35 with a tailwind." Danny aborted a laugh, and Quickdraw McGraw spun and leaned in the window to check the miles I guess. Danny looked at me with eyebrows raised. I shrugged in response, and we both looked away from each other as quickly as Quickdraw – I realized he had never actually said his name – spun back to us. "You got the title?"

"Absolutely." Danny pulled one from his chemistry folder, and I thought, what if the guy happened to see more than one in there? He looked it over, leaned over the windshield to see the VIN under the glass and glanced back and forth a couple times.

"Take it for a turn?"

Danny handed him the keys. "All yours."

As soon as he fired it up, he moaned. "Oh, now. Needs a new muffler."

"Yeah, that's why it's so cheap."

"Cheap, huh? Well." He put it in gear and pulled out of the lot. He rolled down the window and leaned far to that side, I guess listening as he came to a stop or took a turn or accelerated.

"A real work horse."

Quickdraw lifted his chin in reply.

"Y'all say you're from Omaha?"

We both replied, not quite in synch. "Yes." He gave a snort for a laugh, at what, I wasn't sure.

"You can't be too careful with that Craigslist stuff. A while back someone killed a guy who showed up to buy something." Our eyes met in the rearview mirror and I cursed myself for looking there. I feigned a stretch and readjusted in the back seat so I could look out the window while remaining outside the field of the mirror.

Moments later we came into the lot from the other side of the block and pulled up next to his pickup truck. "OK, I know you knocked off for the muffler, but that's still too much. Let's say another hundred off." He wasn't asking. "That rusty back fender... OK. Let's say five hundred. Now, how's this gonna work? Check OK?"

"Cash. Too late to get to the bank and we'll be getting a lift back to Omaha."

"Uh-huh."

"So if it's OK with you, we can follow you back, drop the car, and you can drop us at the Shell truck stop on the interstate?"

"Uh-huh."

I didn't like the tone in his responses. Like he got the answers he expected but doubted each one.

"Got any extra sets of keys?"

I tensed right up and turned to look out the window again. At a poker table that would have blown it.

"Nope, this is it." Danny added, "We can make another set at the truck stop if you need to. My treat."

"Uh-huh. So... you'll follow me home?"

"Yep."

He slipped out of the driver's seat and climbed back into his truck, while I got out of the back and took the passenger seat as Danny walked around the front of the car, appraising it as if he was the buyer or maybe reluctant to let it go. He was really selling his role as much as the car, and I felt a strange longing when he ran his fingers through the flop of hair back from his forehead as if to say "what am I going to do now?" He looked up. "OK, you lead."

We turned down a street with a sign that read No Outlet, lined with generic ranch-style houses but with big yards and good spaces in between them. His lawn needed cutting and was dotted with pine trees and lined on either side with a row of arborvitae. The open garage door revealed no space for a vehicle. There didn't even appear to be a place to walk through all the teetering stacks of boxes, a riding lawn mower, a rusted stove, two refrigerators taped shut with duct tape, and a work table with tools hanging in their outlines along the back wall. He went in through the front door and came back with a wad of twenties. Danny counted them out on the hood of the car and the man smiled at me. "All there?" he asked while staring at me. I didn't understand, but Danny answered, "Yup. Congratulations, you've got yourself a great little car."

NANCY SAT AT the kitchen table, my adequate report card and some pamphlets from the community college laid out like a poker hand she didn't know what to make of. Mr. Sommerset had tapped her elbow in the hall at school that night. "Not urgent yet, of course. She still has about a year to make a plan," he'd said, slipping some info into the hand clutching my grades.

She blew a hard stream of smoke at the kitchen light, like an aging dragon who can't believe she's lost her flame. "You can stay here, you know. I've got your back."

I stood in the doorway to the living room, hiding behind crossed arms, one foot awkwardly crossed before the other. I banged the side of my head against the door frame harder than I intended and it hurt a bit. "Nelsonville? God."

"Or not. You can try to get in at U of I."

"I have no money, Nance. You didn't let me work, remember?"

She shrugged with her eyebrows, drink in one hand. "I will help, of course."

"How? How can you possibly help?"

"Haven't I already?" I stared at the tabletop. "You do what needs to be done," she said, not to me but the general you. "I will always have your back."

The room blurred, and I don't know why this all felt so awkward. I had no quick clever reply.

"What the hell keeps us here anyway?"

She looked up at me then, her head tilted, chin resting on her propped up smoking hand, her face at peace. She didn't stare in my eyes, but seemed to scan my face, searching for something or making sure nothing was missing. The ice in her glass tinkled lightly as she took a long sip, but she didn't look away until I did.

"HE'S CREEPY."

"Ain't a crime."

I scowled at Danny, a bit of mustard in the corner of his mouth, as he wadded up the foil wrapper of his second gas station hot dog that looked like a fat pruney finger.

"I don't want to go back there. Can you do it yourself?"

"Are you shittin' me?"

I said nothing, so he assumed I was, apparently, shitting him. On foot, it took nearly two hours to get out there again, must have been about six miles. We watched the place in silence for a while, then came up the driveway, running in a half-crouch the way commando soldiers slip under the whirling blades of a helicopter. We reached in through the open windows and laid our bags on the back seat. Danny ran around to the front and I opened the driver's door. The dome light came on and my breath caught. In the dim glow I could see Danny's eyes go wide. I jumped into the seat, keys in hand, and before I could close the door, I heard the man's voice from somewhere in the darkness of the garage.

"Brought me a second set of keys?"

Danny stood up and whirled toward the sound.

"Surprised?" He stepped out of the darkness of the garage into the semi-darkness of the drive. I watched for his hands, expecting a gun or something, but his arms remained crossed.

"Look, we don't want trouble. You can have all your money back. Please. We don't mean anything, it's just my grandma..."

"Right. In Florida. I know. Or in Iowa?"

Danny shook his head.

"The one you sold this car to? Saw the story on the internet."

"I can explain. It's—"

"—too fucking late, is what it is. So now... Keys." He held out his hand.

Danny shook his head again like he was trying to rattle out what to do next.

"Keys!"

We both jumped, and I came around the car door and handed them to Danny to pass on.

"OK, now, inside. Go. *March!*"

He pointed and we shuffled along, slouched and terrified, through a flimsy aluminum screen door and into the living room. The drapes were drawn, and a TV sat dark in one corner opposite a defeated couch. One lamp, the shade yellowed and cracked, made everything outside its bright little circle look amber. Old fake-wood paneling covered the walls, sucking up the light and making the room feel like a basement despite the screen door – which he stood before, seething. His eyes wild now, he paced three steps back and forth as if he was uncertain which direction to walk, his fists clenched, breaths coming sharp. I felt the energy of his frenetic movement pass to me as rising panic.

Danny swallowed hard before he could speak. "Look, we can give you the money back. Maybe some extra, too. Please, we are trying to get away from abusive parents."

He lunged into Danny's space, and Danny either fell back or sat down on the couch, so I sat down next to him. "Cut the shit. No one's buying it. I think we call the police."

"No, please!" Anguish rose up in Danny's voice, feigned or real, and he was on his feet again.

"I own you now, asshole. Try to cheat me." He stabbed at the air between them with a forefinger.

"I told you, you can have all the money. Whatever you want."

He thought about that a long second. "Well, then, let's have a little fun here. Whatya say?"

"Please, sir," I heard my own voice, airy and high-pitched, hardly a whisper as I got up and hid behind Danny.

He looked at me. "Show me your breasts."

"What?"

"No fucking way." Danny stepped back into me.

"Fucking way! Show 'em."

"Are you crazy? Just take the money!"

"No, you know what? Blow job. Right here, you little shits."

"You're not touching her."

The man clenched his teeth, but then loosened up with a laugh. "I wasn't talking about the girl."

Danny recoiled like he'd been hit in the face with a two-by-four. "The fuck?"

The man laughed, seeing himself in control of the situation now, "Don't kid yourself, faggot. The little lady." I felt a full-body shiver, and I tried not to let the blur in my eyes spill down my cheeks. He jabbed his finger at me now and swung an arm back behind him, snatching a cordless phone off the lamp table. "Now. Or I call the cops. Jail for stealing cars. Over state lines? That's a real big deal. That's serious time. Or... you make amends."

No longer standing so tall as he had when he played his part, Danny stepped a bit to the side and closer to him, and the man took a short step to his left like they were circling the center of the room. But his eyes locked on me.

"I can't let you do that," said Danny.

The man cackled. "You don't have a choice, asshole. It's that or cops."

"No. Please. Can't we fix this?"

"You have one choice. I *own* you right now."

Danny's head slumped and he didn't move for a long time. Then he stepped back, and there was nothing between me and those crazy eyes.

"Well? What's it gonna be?"

"Diane?" The tone of Danny's voice stopped my heart. He turned to me expectantly. I opened my mouth to speak but couldn't find words. I stepped back, tears overflowing now.

"He's got us, Diane. You heard him. We've got no choice."

"What??" Everything's negotiable.

"And then we walk," he said to the man.

The guy snorted and looked at me in a way I don't ever want to see again. The sobs bubbled up, uncontrollable. "It can be quick, Diane. Ain't nothing. We don't want trouble. Just quick."

I couldn't tell if he spoke to me or the man, but Danny's next words, taunting and sleazy, burned my ears and dropped my stomach. "Well, hot shot? Are we gonna do this? Then we walk. That's the deal."

Without hesitation, the guy whipped it out, already half aroused, and I looked away too late and clenched my eyes shut, falling back even more.

"You, sit where I can see you," he said to Danny, who obliged by backing to the couch, the springs groaning under his weight. I looked back at him, his hands in his pockets, and he didn't even look up at me.

I turned forward, eyes to the floor as I heard the rattle of the belt buckle and the creak of the floor as the man stepped forward. "What's wrong, sweetheart? Don't be shy," he said. I stepped back, my hands trembling and then my whole body, and I felt the couch come up against the backs of my legs. I covered my face, and I heard his dry laugh, the buckle, the floor, another creak of the couch, and... the shutter sound of a camera.

"The fuck--?"

I opened my eyes. He dropped the cordless phone on the carpet and was frantically tugging up his zipper with one hand while reaching for Danny with the other. Danny flew up from the couch and turned his backside into him like he was protecting a basketball. They started to grapple.

"It's done. It's done! I sent it. Back the fuck off!"

"What??" The man whipped him around, and Danny held up his iPhone like he was taunting a kid who's too short.

"I sent the photo."

The man and I both stared at Danny in shock. A fleeting ripple of relief passed through my knees but was gone, like the moment a bus lurches and you re-adjust your footing but remain tensed and off balance: he had no cell service.

"*Now* who's sorry, asshole? Go ahead. Call the cops. We'll take our chances with juvenile court, but see how far you get as a pedophile."

"Fucking liar! Sent it where?"

"Somewhere safe, asshole. You let us go, we treat it as a joke, something I found online."

"You're bullshitting me!"

"Do I look like I am?" His one-sided grin would have sold me if I didn't know he had no bars. But the man faltered and Danny pressed on. "You look a little sick there, cowboy. Now like I said, we ain't looking for trouble. Fair is fair, you caught us. I give you the cash. We walk. You forget about it all, and we forget about *this*." He waved the phone.

"Fuck that. How can I trust you?"

"You can't. And we sure as hell can't trust you either."

He gritted his teeth and clenched both fists but didn't step forward. "My money back, and you delete that right now. And I want to know where you sent it."

"Two out of three." Danny threw down the wad of twenties. "I ain't saying where it went. That's insurance. But..." He thumbed around the screen. "See? Gone." He held the phone up and swiped a few photos as proof.

"And that shot of my fucking house. Delete it."

"OK... done. Sent *that* one before we came here. So don't get any ideas. Someone knows where we are right now."

The man's shoulders sagged, but then heat rose into his face and right about that time we all figured out maybe he did have one other option: kill us. He jumped onto Danny and they fell in a tangle on the floor against the couch. Danny kicked away and held his phone out of reach. "Are you crazy? Get off of me!" The man rolled away and leapt to his feet, Danny's wallet in his hand. He thumbed through and took all the cash. "My money back, plus all this... and your I.D."

We all stood, feet planted, muscles tensed, and his chest rose up and down like he'd been running.

Danny licked his lips, his hand stretched out in the air reaching at empty space. "This ends here. You've got all our money. We can call in the photo if you turn in my I.D. We're square. Are we square?"

"Get the *fuck* out of my house."

I backed into the screen door with a bang, opened it, and stepped out backward. Danny followed. The man didn't appear again in the door, but I could hear him cursing. Danny took another set of keys from his pocket. We got in, and with unbearable calm, he backed out, and we drove away. I wanted to scream. I wanted tires screeching. I wanted to throw up.

WE DROVE IN silence, the pale glow of the dashboard on our faces. I hugged my knees to my chest and kept saying "holy shit" to myself over and over again, the sobs shaking my whole body. Sharp pains in my kidneys gradually weakened. Not even a half hour out of town we pulled into the looping road of a mostly empty county park with self-pay camping. A half dozen dark RVs spread out on the grass, one of them with a little campfire down to embers. Danny found a spot far from the rest near a sprawling oak tree and parked. "Tent?"

I nodded once but couldn't move. He got out and set it all up, and I alternated between tears and bouts of hyperventilating. He tapped on the window, and I got out. We both lay down on top of the sleeping bag in the tent.

"This... that was... Holy shit."

"Don't be ridiculous."

"It was fucking bad! Oh my god, Danny! Do you realize...?"

"Shhhh! Jesus, Diane," he indicated the few campers around us. "I never would have let him touch you."

I believed he believed that, but it didn't really matter. The easy return of his confidence gave me a deep chill. The merest thought of what had just happened, and imagining what *could* have happened, made the spit rise up on my tongue and my stomach warp. He put his fingers up to touch my hair and I flinched. "Don't."

"Jesus. Fine." He rolled over with his back to me. "Nothing happened. I still have most of the money in my backpack. We're OK now. Let it rest."

Rest? And sure as hell, within minutes his breathing slowed and deepened.

IT TOOK ME over two hours to walk back toward town, and, after asking at a couple of service stations, another hour to find my way to a gas station right off the interstate with a Greyhound logo in the window. I laid down the hundred-dollar bill from Danny's backpack. The kid at the counter said, "I need an I.D." I made no move to offer one. I just stared and let the tears stream again, and he looked away. Outside, a row of motel rooms stood along the edge of the wide parking lot. I wondered if Danny would come looking for me, if he'd guess where I'd have gone.

I sat on the concrete outside the door, next to an ice cooler padlocked against people who would steal ice cubes, I guess, and clutched the ticket in my hand. Two hours later the bus rolled in. The driver looked me up and down. "No bags?"

"Nope." I found my seat and stayed awake for a few hours, eating corn nuts one at a time to make them last and watching recently familiar town names go past in reverse as I kept some sort of midnight vigil. Only when the pink glow of the next day graced the horizon before us did my eyelids lose the fight with sleep. I thought of my bed then and wondered what my mother's reaction was going to be and if she had reported me missing. I imagined her voice, as I slipped into nothingness: you win some, you lose some.

The Butcher Boys

IN RETELLINGS, IT GREW to an epic takedown story over the years. But truth be told, the time the Butcher Boys delivered the pain to Bobby Kurtz was anti-climactic and came as an epilogue. The tale's elevation to legend can probably be attributed to the fact that no one wanted to talk about when William disappeared, which happened about the same time.

Bobby lived a couple blocks down the street from the rest of us, but we all went to the same school. He tripped you on the playground when the bell rang after recess. He knocked books out of your hands in class or trays at lunch. He "Jap slapped" you – coming up behind you to clap his hands hard over your ears on either side of your head, making them ring for half an hour. He sucker punched and pulled wedgies; threw rocks, crab apples, and citrus-smelling black walnuts that stung like nothing else. He applied headlocks and sleeper holds until you saw stars. And then, as you sat defeated on the pavement in tears, he laughed over you. It was endless, and, as much as we feared him, we also found the whole process tedious and inevitable. Then, like a plague lifting, he moved away. Bobby's father blessed the neighborhood when he found work down state, and peace came to the last couple blocks on North Birch Street.

Then a year later, Bobby's folks came back to town to visit and left him to wander down the street looking for old trouble. He found it when he met the new kids in town.

About a month after the Kurtzes had moved, the Butcher Boys and their father – but no mother – had moved into The Old Widow's house at the top of our block; the actual owners, possibly descendents, lived somewhere down in Florida. After years of leaving it abandoned, they had decided to rent it, with the expectation that the new occupants would clean it up in exchange for discounted rent. The Old Widow had passed on before most of the neighborhood kids had been born, but that house sat empty, an ominous gloom hanging over it for years, so that none of us even ventured to snag wormy apples from the sagging trees at the corner of the lot. The house itself looked on with darkened windows through a gap in some tall pines standing like sentries scratching at the windows of a front porch filled with boxes, a rotting sofa, and ruined antiques.

Life seems contrived sometimes, in particular when surnames seemingly dictate one's fate. We had a dentist in town named Dr.

Smiley and, kid you not, an orthopedic surgeon, Dr. Bonebrake. But while the Butcher Boys, Paul and Mike, weren't brutal bullies, they boxed, trained at a gym, and had fought in the Silver Gloves competition before the move up from Chicago. Like many people properly trained to fight, they learned to respect their superpower. And their reputation – and perhaps their name – meant they rarely needed to use it.

This was the summer before we started middle school. We boys were a couple years younger than Paul Butcher, who in turn was two years junior to his brother Mike, who attended high school as a sophomore, though he may have been held back a year, they say. Sam Skoronski, Dave Peterson, Greg Miller and I were the first round of sons in a street of drafty 1930s bungalows taken over by young couples who'd found their first homes and still could tell you what trunk in the attic had a wedding dress and where their box of high-school LPs was.

By this time, we hadn't outgrown kick-the-can, but wouldn't allow our younger brothers and sisters to tag along anymore on shenanigans for fear of them naively reporting back to our parents. Greg's six-year-old little brother, William, small enough that any of us could easily swing him over a shoulder like a sack of potatoes, was a direct hotline to the Miller residence, and from there dispatches went out, sooner or later, to the rest of our parents. Try as we might to shake him, he always found us.

The only other kid our age was Donnie Lewis, a couple sizes bigger than us all but mentally functioning about two years shy of William. Donnie didn't talk so much as moan or grunt from time to time, but he helped fill the field for baseball. We didn't pick on Donnie directly, but sometimes we'd call William "George" the way the big slow character in a Daffy Duck cartoon referred to the little companion he followed around. I guess we were still being mean, but at least we were subtle and indirect about it.

Donnie's parents lived on the next street over in a small house behind the only white picket fence I'd ever seen outside of television. About ten or fifteen years older than our parents, they'd had Donnie pretty late in life. Mrs. Lewis made the best peanut butter cookies with the fork marks across the back, treating us to them often, grateful I think that we included Donnie in games.

A typical summer day, all of us gathered in the empty lot next door to The Old Widow's place to play some ball. I stood lazy-waving a Louisville slugger older than any of us. Donnie stood straight-legged behind the plate, the permanent and reliable catcher who would only throw directly back to the stacked sod that functioned as a mound. You had to pay attention to Donnie: it didn't matter if you were looking or no one was there to catch it – Donnie threw to the mound. He'd throw it right through you if you stood in the way. He had his target to focus on and everything else was peripheral and irrelevant. The rest of us were out in the field waiting to be called in to take our turns at bat. Greg started his windup but suddenly came down flat-footed, his arms dangling at his sides as he stared off the field toward the street.

"That's a balk!" shouted Sam from left field. But Greg didn't budge, and one by one we all turned and looked across the street to see Bobby Kurtz standing on the walk, arms crossed. We all froze, our heads up like deer when they first sense the wolf at the edge of the field. That is, except Paul and Mike.

"What gives? Are we playing ball or statue maker?"

I stood at second/short center, closest to shortstop Mike, and spoke from behind my glove. "That's Bobby. You know. The guy we told you about. Used to mess with us."

He snorted, made some signal I couldn't see to Paul, and walked over like the manager coming in to change the pitcher. Paul followed in step. The Butcher Boys, lithe and loose, strolled across the street.

"Who the hell are you?" Bobby stood a couple inches taller than both of them, but his lack of wariness surprised me.

"We just wanna talk."

The Butcher Boys didn't split to either side for a strategic advantage as they approached; they just stood together right in front of Bobby, completely relaxed. Mike did the talking as we gathered at the opposite curb behind them. We couldn't hear everything. Mike spoke softly and pointed a thumb over his shoulder in our direction. Talking didn't last long. Bobby threw his hand forward at Paul. Not a punch but more like an attempted slap. Paul turned his face and leaned back and right without even lifting his fists to block it, like Muhammad Ali. The groping fingers found only air. Mike looked down at Bobby's feet and shook his head like my father did to me when he was disappointed.

Then a dull smack of skin, a thud of bone meeting resistance so fast we weren't sure we'd seen it. Bobby staggered back several paces, managing to keep his feet but his arms waving for balance. Blood already paved the way from his nose to his lip. And that was it, we thought. With a single punch, Paul Butcher put the final punctuation mark on an era that we had already figured ended the year before. He removed a title. But Paul wasn't finished. He went in with a couple hard punches to Bobby's stomach, then lifted Bobby's head a bit and dropped another across the nose, maybe looking to break it. Mike laid a hand gently on Paul's elbow and said, "Hey."

Bobby, folded up a bit, started crab-walking down the street toward his former home. He waited until he had some distance before he shouted – shocking us all – "Fuck you!" Paul stepped forward and stamped his foot on the walk, and Bobby turned and picked up his pace. The Butcher Boys laughed and the rest of us joined them nervously. We went back to our positions, waving our arms like Bobby had, and baseball resumed as if the whole thing had been a seventh-inning stretch.

MR. BUTCHER – even my father referred to him as such – worked as a machinist at a factory on the south side of town. My father used first names for all other neighbors when talking to my mother, while we, as children who were taught respect, never dared. So hearing him refer to the man as "Mister" with my mother added to the mystique.

Mr. Butcher had a bum right leg, the shoe pointed stubbornly to the inside. When he walked, he dragged it forward and planted it as if he were trying to trip himself. Sam claimed it happened early in Vietnam, and we eagerly believed that, but more likely it was congenital or a really bad childhood accident. No one asked, of course, but happily speculated. He stood a few inches shorter than his sons, but their quiet deference made it seem as if they looked up to him even physically.

Out on the gravel driveway, Mr. Butcher kept a pickup

truck with a camper mounted in the bed. Behind the house, the garage leaned as if waiting for a bus. Inside was a 1948 Ford coupe, the remaining black paint dull like lump charcoal. As if washed up on a beach, it sat on four flats under the weight of years of dust and rust. My father had seen it in action, though I never imagined when or why, and he told me, "The Old Widow must not have had kids. Only two doors, the coupe."

On the opposite side of the garage stood a work bench with some tools and scattered screws, nuts, fasteners, metal shavings and nails littering the oil-stained wooden surface. The only light came through the garage door windows, nearly opaque with grime, and the odd spaces between planks in the walls. An overgrown garden to the right of the garage, separating the property's big yard from the empty baseball lot, functioned as a graveyard for more junk: a couple of skeletal lawnmowers, a concrete bird bath stained and stagnant, a beat up couch decayed down to springs, an old toilet which we found funny and posed upon as The Thinker for a giggle. A rusting refrigerator stood planted in the mud, waiting to serve, and part of some kind of plow looked as if it had died in action, leaving us to ponder if it had been dumped there or if the neighborhood had risen up around the ruins of an old farm house. A large metal barrel, with patches and chips of blue paint seemingly holding the rusted thing together, gathered rainwater under the broken downspout at the back corner of the garage beneath the mossy edge of the eaves and shingles. At his father's instruction, Paul set up a live trap back there in an ongoing war with raccoons and squirrels. Some of them ended up dead and stinking; the others presumably were given a lift to the city limits—or ended up dead but out of sight.

Paul showed us treasures: old beer cans with rusted peaked tops like oil cans; a hand-powered drill that operated with a little crank like an egg beater; large metal bearings that we mistook for marbles, "steelies" we called them, outranking in play anything made of glass; and, putting the hush to our voices, a copy of a girly magazine, tattered and rippled with water damage. Paul took it from its hiding place in the icebox of the old fridge in the yard for us once, laid it across the work table in the half light, and we learned anatomy never taught in school. Mostly photos of naked women, but one series showed a couple frozen in some unearthly dance step or wrestling maneuver. Tangled in a variety of confusing poses across the matching curves of a sporty yellow Corvette, they roused something almost as confusing in us. Paul turned pages and stepped back so we could see. We all blinked at one shot of the two with their faces hanging over each others' private parts. "Blow job," Paul nodded, our sage instructor.

"Why would you want to blow on someone like that?" Greg asked.

"That's not what they're doing there, Greg," said Paul. "You'll understand some day... When you're fifty maybe." He laughed knowingly, and the rest of us joined a beat later, each of us, I think, secretly certain we were the only ones who didn't get it.

"Greg! Mom says you gotta come home." Greg's little brother, William, had a piercing voice. Paul folded up anatomy class, and Greg, scowling, shouted to be heard outside the garage. "I'm coming. Tell her, I'll be right there."

William appeared in the side door, Donnie in tow. "But she said—"

"Go on. Beat it!" Hunched up, he turned to go. Donnie stared past us at the magazine on the table until William, speaking over his shoulder, said "Come on, Donnie."

Greg would remember that moment with regret, though it wasn't the last thing he'd said before his brother went missing.

AFTER SUPPER WE headed out on our bikes to ride the trails that angled up and down the deep cut of the ravine where the trains entered town from the north. My father shouted after me, "Be back in an hour. I need you in this street before dark!"

We had more than an hour then. Summer sunsets came late. Even on Fourth of July, the firefighters tasked to light up the celebration waited until after 9 for a sufficiently darkened sky. We rode up the street, and I could see the Butcher Boys sparring with each other out back near the garage. Every practice punch was enough to lay any one of us out, but Mike caught each one in his open palm without fail, the same way he played shortstop.

At the end of our block, Birch crossed Hamilton Street and continued past three more houses on either side. Then the pavement ended as if someone had never finished the road. Past there the land descended into tangled foliage, and the tops of the trees below reached up just barely higher than our heads at street level. Sam raced straight into the brush, down a line of packed dirt toward the railroad tracks, and I followed behind him, pressing the pedals backward to ride the brake to the bottom. I caught up to him on the flats running alongside and slightly below the rails and their bed of crushed stone. We ran our toys through the gauntlet, the rugged terrain bullying our bikes made for sidewalks and asphalt. The week before, Greg had punctured a tire on a stray piece of granite, and we ribbed him, contributing the mishap to his chubbiness. We helped him carry the bike home so his father could sink the tube in a bucket of water to find the leak and apply a duct tape fix.

A band of trees and brush lined the town side of the ravine, while a full forest began along the top of the other side. We'd balance along a dusty line, bobbing over earthy waves, with buckthorn branches and blackcap brambles snagging at our sleeves as we passed. Our crisscrossing web of trails stayed close to the ravine as the forest beyond became deeper and the ground more rugged, strewn with the rotting, moss-covered trunks of yesteryear's oaks and maples.

Tiring of that circuit, we zipped back down into the ravine. Sam stopped up ahead, and, as I slowed, Dave came up alongside me. Greg caught up a beat later. "Why'd you stop?" he asked. Sam put down his kickstand, dismounted, and balanced the bike gently in the dirt, pausing with his hands over the handlebars as one did when building a card castle, careful not to release it too soon. He disappeared into the brush. "Come see this!"

Dave and I stood our bikes -- Greg dumped his -- and we followed. We found Sam poking at something with a long stick: a dead raccoon cut in half.

"Whoa!" "Gross!" "Holy crap!"

Sam turned with a smile that expressed both disgust and incredulity, our host for amateur Ripley's *Believe It or Not*. "Clean in half!"

"Train got him," said Dave, stating the obvious.

Sam rolled it over with the stick and its tiny, sharp teeth clenched in a grimace, as if in the last second of life the poor animal had cringed at its certain fate as the light of the engine fixed him and the thunder of death followed.

"It smells like when I didn't take the trash out from under the sink for a couple days after burger night," Sam laughed. "Yuck! Dad got pretty mad."

"Same thing," I said. "Dead meat!"

On cue the long plaintive wail of one of the evening trains came from far off. Our heads went up like prairie dogs, Sam dropped the stick, and as if by silent command, we all ran up the stones and lay our heads on the tracks to listen like we'd seen in Westerns on WGN, a channel out of Chicago that we could only watch at Sam's as his family had cable TV.

The earth shook as an iron horse stampede rounded the bend before entering town; we stepped back to give it respectful distance. We'd already heard stories, but that raccoon made them stick. We waved and reached in the air to pull down the invisible cord, the one we knew truck drivers, and we assumed the engineers, used to blare their horns. He waved back and gave four blasts that made our guts quiver -- two short, one long, one short, required each of the road crossings through town. The trains, some a mile long, barely slowed for our little city, setting off flashing red lights, bells, and barricades as they raced through with a roar and trailed a rapid double-tapping rhythm of steel, a giant's hammer on an anvil. We waited out the train, rode for a bit more, and then dutifully headed home before dusk gathered.

THOSE TWO BLOCKS on a residential street felt like the entire world. I remember my small place in life as orderly. Fathers left for work in the morning, returned for dinner prepared by stay-at-home mothers. Sensible cars parked in the drives. Each house getting its turn for a new shingled roof and then aluminum siding. Black and white TVs, giving way to fancy colored models, dignified like furniture in the corners of our living rooms. While I have memories of free time and play, favorite shows and favored games, it all happened within a framework: bed times, supper times, homework, school-night rules, weekend curfews.

Our household was no exception, but we didn't quite fit in the squares, like a foundation that sagged unseen and set the front porch off kilter. My mother was working as a bookkeeper when she met my father. They married and had just one child, not two, and when she felt I could come home on my own with enough sense not to set the house on fire or invite a creepy stranger in, she went back to work part-time doing the books for a local hardware store. She thought about expanding her earnings by making a deal with the owner and taking on non-competitive clients on her own. My father liked the idea but as I lurked around the edges of adult conversations, I sensed tension from the topic. I overheard bits and pieces when Mrs. Peterson – Dave's mom – brought over a coffee cake and they gossiped on the porch with a pot of Maxwell House. The other moms half-smiled when my mother brought it up, showing either unsettled surprise or a conspiratorial thrill of hearing something not fit for public consumption.

The same hushed tones for the single mother who worked at the hardware store. The older, married owners with two adult children seemed to hover over her like a refugee who needed saving. Never mind that the housewives had no idea what to think of Mr. Butcher, a single dad. "Things change," my mom would say. The others would raise their eyebrows and nod into their coffee cups. I confess I had a secret pride in our being different, and I know as an only child I never had to share my parents' attentions.

IT WAS A FRIDAY in July. The Butchers had packed up for a trip and left in the middle of the afternoon, so we played no baseball. The sun seemed to sear the ground recalling a black-and-white Flash Gordon rerun I'd seen weeks before in its Saturday afternoon time slot. A cliffhanger. Flash was ambushed in a forest of ghost trees and pinned down by a blazing heat ray. We wondered why he didn't simply roll left or right, or duck behind one of the naked trunks. The heat that day made me commiserate, and none of us dared venture into the light, sagging like sacks of potatoes in the shade where the humidity still reached us and left us listless. Sam, Greg, Dave, and I sat in the shade at a picnic table behind Dave's house where his mother served us lime Kool-Aid without enough sugar in it while we played Monopoly, slipping our colored money stashes under the edge of the board to protect them from a gathering breeze. Dave got called in to help with something, and the rest of us wandered off down the open backyards, a sort of no-man's land, a green corridor we kids used as often as the front sidewalk.

Finally, the five o'clock calls came round for supper. My own folks never started cooking until after the news, so I lingered longer under a sugar maple that marked the corner of four lots. Greg didn't answer the supper call until finally his father walked two houses down to find him.

"Where's your brother?"

Greg shrugged. "I dunno."

"Well, go find him. Time for supper."

Greg's face sagged into a frown and his body seemed to follow with it, limbs rubbery and weak, head lolling off to one side. We all did that, hoping without hope that we might be relieved of a task for our sudden and complete palsy.

Greg set off toward the street. I could hear him calling, drawing out his brother's name like a cat moaning in an alley, until it slipped beneath the susurrus of the leaves, and the rising and falling buzz of cicadas. I watched ants like a fire brigade, passing each other along an invisible trail through a patch of packed dirt, pausing to exchange antenna greetings. I tried to divert some with blades of grass. Then I smeared their little circular portal of sand, and they immediately went into action clearing out the hole once again. So industrious.

Mr. Miller's shouting for Greg woke me from the ant world. Only then did I realize a lot of time had passed. He came back to the tree with an urgency that made me nervous.

"Andy, have you seen Greg?"

"Yes, sir. He went up the street a while ago."

"And William?"

"No, sir."

He stood a moment, hands on his hips, staring down as if he too saw an anthill. Then he turned on a heel and headed back to his house. He backed the car out of the drive and headed up the street. I wasn't sure why he didn't walk. Greg couldn't have gone far.

I answered my own dinnertime summons finally and went inside to eat, an odd cheesy rice sort of chicken casserole my mom prided herself on. Afterward, the three of us watched the Carol Burnett Show, laughing with the rest of the cast unable to stay in character through a skit with Tim Conway. Then we retired to the front porch. My father came out singing the end theme in a mock opera voice, "I'm so glad we had this time together..." with a bottle of Old Milwaukee beer in hand. He sat next to my mother on the wicker loveseat and leaned forward with his tie loosened, sleeves rolled up, and elbows on his knees like he was watching a ballgame. Mom crossed her legs and bounced her foot at the ankle, her hand resting on his shoulder. No one spoke; just us listening to the drone of cicadas, voices on a television across the street, birds making one last twittering songfest as the sun dwindled somewhere up the street and beyond the houses already hunkering down in the shadows of century-old maples and black walnut trees.

Mr. Miller drove past; Greg in the passenger seat didn't even look up at us. They pulled into their yard, and we heard the car doors on the other side of the house as Mr. Miller shouted to his wife. Greg came over at a half run. "We can't find William."

THE URGENCY TOOK us off guard, like storm sirens on a sunny day. We didn't assume the worst in those days. The call to alarm, the panic and fear rose slowly like a pot of cold water on an old stove. We assumed innocence first: someone's tardy, lost track of time, maybe pouting and running away all of two blocks from home to return an hour later, the Prodigal Son. Not like now with Amber alerts and a continuous news cycle of all the atrocities and abductions and pedophiles that plagued every town from here to Timbuktu going back three decades even in televised docudramas. Bad things happened then, surely, but we weren't always present for it, and most of it never reached our ears. And the rare story that did get legs often remained a mystery, emerging years later with our obsession with cold cases.

My father, Mr. Peterson, Mr. Skoronski and the Millers set off in the cardinal directions searching a growing circle of territory. I begged to join, and, with a moment's hesitation, my father consented. Mr. Miller returned to the north and the railroad tracks. But everyone circled back home after a couple hours.

Mr. Miller called the police, and they didn't offer niceties or put off a search for 24 hours as a wait-and-see approach. A patrol car showed up in the Millers' drive in minutes. All of us brought out flashlights and, for lack of places to look, headed back to the woods, while mothers paired up and walked up and down the street grid calling into the backyards, pausing here and there in front of houses of certain unknown neighbors or, frankly, any place that resembled the Old Widow's, trying to push back the thought that another being was involved.

How far could a little boy get on his own? Wouldn't he be wailing in tears? While the rural world lay beyond the end of our street, county highways, gravel roads, open fields, and farmhouses were never far from sight. Wouldn't William wander down a road at some point? But would a stranger know he was in trouble? Would William, in childlike caution and shyness, avoid strangers or passing cars? Anxiety mounted, but I think we all still refused to believe it possible he had gone far. Lost or fallen down a ditch with a twisted ankle maybe.

The search started again early the next day, the initial adrenaline giving way to a quivering feeling in the pits of my stomach as the sun moved too quickly across the sky. The county sheriff had gotten involved by late morning, expanding the search, and the story went statewide on the evening news, which we watched while devouring sandwiches in the living room before heading back out.

By day four it felt as if the hourglass ran out. What could be done other than pace in a circle. No place remained to be searched. If he had been kidnapped, as we increasingly believed but never would admit aloud, then he could have been taken over state lines by this time. So now the days went back to being long again. Then weeks bled away, devoid of joy, heavy and listless. I'd call it an atmosphere of mourning but even that possesses certainty.

MEMORY STRETCHES summer days longer with nostalgia, with a sense of innocence and delusions of immortality. The music was better, the weather, the friends, the fun, and never a dull duty or routine that could press the days into identical shapes. I try to think of the specific highlights now, but eventually I come back to the blunt emotional weight of that summer. Just long days treading every square inch of town and farther out, in concentric squares and circles, into the farms, cornfields, forests, and on into neighboring towns. Not so much as a possible sighting or a workable theory, a hint of William. Police officers and volunteers knocked on every door. Handbills stapled to telephone poles along the block smacked of desperation; no one with even an iota of attention could possibly not have heard the news and understood the desperate search.

What if he didn't come back? What did that even mean and how was that even something to think about? People could be hurt, they could get sick, they could even die – the neighborhood had already seen off Mr. Bachman down the street after a heart attack, a few of our great grandparents, and a fellow in a motorcycle crash who lived out by the feed mill a mile out of town. Death had introduced itself to our young minds, but no one simply disappeared without a trace.

William slipped away into limbo, and the rest of the neighborhood followed, unsure how to feel or express thoughts or even have conversations. Chatting about the weather over the backyard fence with a neighbor rang hollow. No one laughed loud, even at Carol Burnett or Tim Conway. Eventually we gathered back at the baseball field. No chatter in the outfield; taking the bases at a shuffle. Even Paul Butcher seemed sullen. Mike wasn't around much, he told us. He'd just gotten his driver's license that summer and had a girlfriend now. We saw a blond, freckled girl, tall and awkward, pull into the driveway with her parents' station wagon, sliding across the front seat to let Mike drive.

Greg rarely showed up for games or to ride the trails. When he did none of us knew what to say. We stood unable to meet his eye, surely making him feel more disconnected, adrift, as if he'd lost more than his brother. In fact, he lost his parents, who sat silently apart from each other on the front porch or moved about the yard without direction as if they'd forgotten why they'd stepped outside. Only Donnie remained oblivious to it all, a silver lining to his condition, tossing that ball back to the mound with such focus and care. Nothing else in the world mattered for him outside the minute at hand.

But for Sam, Dave, and I – and especially for Greg – nothing we did at any particular moment meant a damn thing. Without William's nagging call, without Donnie following like a shadow, the air had been sucked right out of our neighborhood.

July had passed, and the first couple weeks of August brought a heat wave with humidity that lay upon us like the lead blanket at the dentist office. Too hot for baseball. We shuffled up the sidewalk toward the Old Widow's House, Sam tapping a fallen maple branch before him, leading us like a blind man, with Greg several paces behind Dave and me.

We plucked a couple of still green crabapples each as we passed under the low-hanging branches. I bit at mine, feeling the sour-bitter juice tighten up my tongue before spitting out a white crescent moon into grass overdue for mowing. We rapped on the front door, the glass panes rattling in the frames, then went around back to knock again. The truck was gone. I scratched at the peeling paint along the railing of the back stoop, as we all stood waiting for each other to decide what to do next, half-hoping perhaps a sleepy Butcher boy might come late to the door. On another day the neighbors should have been hearing the crack of a bat, the jeers from pleasantly bored outfielders. And William. Either squinting at us from right field or returning from the house to fetch Greg for dinner.

Sam crossed the loose gravel to the garage, kicking a larger stone out of his path and dinging it off the rain barrel. He stopped, his hand on the utility door, and turned to us with nose crinkled. "Gah! Another dead coon!"

"What's the point of a live trap if you just let animals die in them?" I asked.

We followed Sam around the corner of the garage and stopped. The trap lay empty, with the wire door poised for the unsuspecting trespasser. We set about searching for the raccoon with our noses, spreading out into the junk piles, circling uncertainly like amateur bloodhounds, moving east, into the breeze. Greg lifted an old car hood in the dirt with one foot and leaned a bit to look. Dave kicked over an empty bucket. Sam swung his foot back and forth over the patches of tall grass, too cautious to step into it. And I came round to the refrigerator, a guilty urge to get another look at its forbidden treasure.

I stopped where the grass before it lay flat and dried out, straw-like in the sun where the discarded wire shelves held it down. I raised my eyes to the fridge itself, the dead animal smell stronger than ever. From the bottom of the door, dark, putrid liquid traced two streaks over the beige paint and stained the grass and earth where it had pooled, soaked in, and dried. I couldn't move, and breathing through my mouth, I fought the urge to wretch.

The others noticed and sidled up without a word. Greg was last. "Find it?" he asked. I turned to him in a panic and he looked at the fridge and made the same calculations in his head. His face broke in horror and he leaped to the door handle as I shouted, "No!"

PARENTS WHOSE CHILDREN go missing hang on to hope, perhaps well beyond the point of reason. You see in the news when a body is found a sense of release, not an end but the beginning of another road of suffering, that of mourning. Everyone, they say, just wants closure. Then it comes, and the grief is drawn to a sharp point. A funeral for a child is an injustice, a life clipped before it had really been given wings. A closed coffin added a sense of erasure as if he still hadn't really been found. A framed photo of William in a little plaid jacket, posed before a mottled sky blue background at the local JC Penney's, rested atop a heartbreakingly small coffin. But what I saw -- what we all saw -- that day would haunt us forever. For weeks I awoke from nightmares, and while Greg never said so, I know he did, too.

The stifling air of the funeral home had followed us out into a world changed, descending like a pox upon all houses. In the cemetery we gathered around the gaping hole that would swallow William up forever. Mr. Miller trembled as he leaned over and let slip a handful of dusty earth.

The Butchers moved away within the month, when the factory shut down. Sam left two years later when his father came down with lung cancer and his mother, in a move that surprised us all, took on an accounting job at a Minnesota-based insurance company with the intention of being closer to Mayo Clinic for treatment. Dave graduated with me from high school, but they'd left the block to move into a simple ranch on the east side of town in a new development, a solutionless maze of cul-de-sacs and yards without empty lots for baseball nor any trees as tall as a rooftop.

And then the Millers. The pain of losing sweet William drove them apart as such a tragedy often does. They divorced less than two years later, and both remarried and moved away by Greg's senior year. He stayed with an aunt to finish but never graduated. He'd fallen in with some rougher kids along the edge, the ones sneaking cigarettes across the street from school, trailing rumors and assumptions, and talk of drugs and alcohol. Bitter and sullen kids they were, and even when Greg laughed among them it looked a lie. After he dropped out, he stayed on in town, and after a bumpy ten years or so, found stability as an office worker at a local company.

The tragedy led to a brief citywide, and ultimately, statewide campaign to remove doors from discarded refrigerators, particularly the old-style models with the latching handles. Years later, after college, marriages, kids, and a couple divorces, the four of us came together every couple years over beers. When the Butcher Boys came up in reminiscing, we all paused, until someone cleared their throat and pushed back against the silence. "Remember that time when the Butcher Boys beat up Bobby Kurtz?"

I moved away for college, and after graduation, took a job at a publishing company in Chicago that produced educational materials – classroom workbooks, textbooks, maps, and the like. My parents, in love with that simple small-town life, left the neighborhood, but moved to another old house they worked on for the better part of a decade on the north end of Main Street. I spoke with them weekly on the phone and returned to visit two or three times a year, never thinking of the house as "home."

Once, I took a drive through the old neighborhood. A new

generation of young parents had taken over and their kids played in sunny yards where the old-growth maples, oaks, and black walnut trees had been cut down. The road itself now had a bridge at the end, crossing the overgrown ravine into a new subdivision where once the forest stood. The Old Widow's House had been fully renovated and not even the stumps remained from the misshapen apple trees and encroaching pines. A new garage stood closer to the street at the end of a paved driveway, and the lawn showed the neat diagonal cuts of a careful mower. Next door, the center of a new house stood squarely on second base. I never drove through there again.

The fate of the Butcher Boys remained a mystery until the dawn of the internet, and I would get the occasional urge to try to find evidence of them online. But I only ever found Paul. He had landed a couple hours away from our hometown, married and with a boy of his own. Now, however, he resided in a ten-by-ten-foot cell at the state penitentiary. I found a short progression of articles that first briefly listed him as an arrest and eventually laid out his life story as a way of explaining how he came to kill his own child, pictured. I couldn't look at the smiling school photo with the clip-on tie and not think of William.

Paul had made a strict father, always about discipline, lacking tolerance for deviation from the rules. Maybe his own father had been the same. I looked at Mike and Paul's reverence around Mr. Butcher with a different sense of possibilities. Paul's youngest – Bill, I noted – had already had a couple trips to the emergency room for "accidents" and a broken arm once. Suspicions had been aroused but no one effectively followed up. Bill was six when he disobeyed his father one last time, taking out his bike from which he had been grounded. As punishment, his father had locked him in the attic to let him think about his errors. I remembered how hot those arched, closed spaces were back on Birch Street. I sweated up in ours, playing around boxes and digging through my parents' memorabilia, a box of old books, a set of fancy French doors they'd never put back in the dining room when they first bought the house. I'd linger until the suffocating heat filled my lungs like warm water, and then I'd climb back down to the kitchen, a bit lightheaded, stepping into the instant relief.

Bill wasn't able to do that, and Paul left him locked up there too long. By the time Paul thought to either let him out or at least deliver some water, Bill had lost consciousness. He died later that night in the hospital. His wife Helen divorced him and left the state, while Paul received fifteen years in prison, where he eventually died of cancer.

The imagination loves a good plot: the Kennedy assassination, Hoffa's disappearance. We believe in farfetched stories to infuse a worthy bit of drama into what really are stupid accidents or meaningless ends. Rather than feeling helpless, it is easier to think someone or something is in control. William's brief pulse of life, ending in a tiny box, is a story only some of us will still remember, yet one of many ephemeral lives marked by fields of headstones, named yet anonymous with time.

The years created a safe distance, and I finally started pondering what we'd all avoided thinking about before. How or why had William ever closed the fridge door on himself? Why didn't anyone hear his pounding or his muffled cries? Right there in the Butchers' back yard. What if someone... what if Paul... Would it be easier if a stupid accident was actually an evil act? The Butchers had left for a couple weeks when William disappeared; and they left for good soon after.

I imagined Bill, and maybe William, each being punished, locked away for having angered Paul. And then Paul and those calculated punches as he toyed with Bobbie Kurtz before Mike stopped him. I thought about going back again, driving the street once more, as if I might find clues in a place that didn't even exist anymore.

Then, as if by fate, I received my invitation: my mother called to tell me Donnie Lewis had passed away. He had outlived his father, but Mrs. Lewis still resided at an assisted-care facility. My mother, always a caring soul, stopped in to visit her once a week. I knew that but I hadn't known that Donnie had lived for years with a certain amount of independence in the house in which he'd been raised. Mrs. Lewis asked my mother if she could help clear out the house, and so I took a long weekend and drove north, the thoughts of Paul as some sort of secretly sadistic neighborhood kid kicking around the back of my brain.

Always the type to get right down to business, my mother didn't even let me unpack. We went directly to the Lewis house, and I planned to take a walk up the street past the old houses when we finished.

We set furniture out on the curb for the local resale shop to pick up, then moved through the other rooms. My mom had had a dumpster delivered, and it rested in the front yard next to the drive. We started filling it with boxes, mostly of clothes and odds and ends we didn't care to sort through.

"Ma, did you ever hear what happened to Paul Butcher?"

She had but hadn't followed the story closely at the time and never thought to tell me. "They left when you were still in middle school. I wasn't even sure you'd remember them."

"We should walk up there."

"Oh, it's all gone. The house is remodeled into an upper and lower, the garage is gone, the lot – remember where you played ball? – another house."

"Yeah, Ma, I know." I suddenly felt foolish, and decided I wouldn't share my wild theory yet.

I emptied a suitcase full of moldy clothing into the dumpster, examined the case, and tossed that out on top of the rest, too. Back in Donnie's room I found his old baseball glove on the top shelf of the closet. He had a single *Star Wars* poster on the wall, faded and torn in a couple places, a giveaway promotion I seem to remember from a local burger franchise. A bookshelf with a collection of children's books also held a couple trophies from high school years that said nothing but second and third place. We didn't have class together with people like Donnie back in those days; they were kept unseen except at lunch when they'd all sit together, ostracized I think now, in a corner with a couple of dedicated staff who looked after them and presumably taught them skills enough that Donnie could live alone here. His last job had been janitorial at the same assisted living center where his mother now stayed.

His room, much like the rest of the house, held a menagerie of little odds and ends, gumball-machine prizes, Happy Meal or cereal box toys, a dozen troll dolls with rainbow-colored hair, a framed photo of his parents from years ago, maybe the 1990s. A wooden desk, much too small for big Donnie, stood against the wall beneath the window to the backyard. A large glass jar full of marbles acted as a bookend for a birding book, a child's picture book about dinosaurs, and a Doctor Seuss collection, with a stockpile of scrap paper in a empty case of green beans from the supermarket holding up the other end. A pair of binoculars with an eyepiece missing, and several tin cans full of pens, colored pencils, crayons, and markers lined the edge of the desktop. The center drawer held a collection of hundreds of key chains. Did we ever really see Donnie?

From the closet, I pulled down a box of clothes so small he couldn't possibly have worn them even in middle school; they smelled of mold and mildew. I headed for the dumpster.

Mom followed me outside, reached into the box she carried, and held up a mass that appeared stuck together. "Baseball cards. Worth something?"

"Jeez, I don't know. I doubt it. But maybe leave them for the resale shop. They'd either chuck them or find out if they are worth something. I can't imagine though."

She shrugged, handed me the box, and returned to the house.

I dumped the cards, and then shook out a couple old school workbooks and papers at the bottom of the box. Something stuck partly under the flap and I reached in to pull it out, holding it before me as I let the box drop. I froze. My hands clenched an old magazine, the cover torn off, a busy table of contents, stained and crumpled. In the flash of a second, I knew what it was. A beat later my eyes confirmed the gut, and my mother walked over and tossed another box over the edge. "What is it? Oh, gosh, you boys. Always comes back to that, doesn't it?" She laughed with derision, waved me away as she turned and headed back into the house.

I pulled the pages apart. The fleshy images, the erotic poses, the yellow Corvette. I heard blood rushing in my ears and realized I was holding my breath.

"Hey, are ya helping? Get over that thing and throw it away. Still got the kitchen to sort out."

I nodded, partly to her, but then stood motionless while my mind raced. Coincidence, I told myself. Something Donnie picked up some random moment before the accident, eyes on the prize and focused, and carried it home. What, when he wasn't shadowing William? The door closed maybe on its own. But the wire shelves in the grass. Playing a game? An accident? Would Donnie have understood if he was there? Did he behave strangely? I tried to remember him those weeks when William remained missing, but I didn't remember a single damn thing. Donnie lived 55 years, and everything that remained of his life lay there in that bin. Roughly 50 more years than William had, half a century in exchange for a peek at a girly magazine? I leaned a hand on the rough metal of the dumpster, staring down into the scattered remnants of Donnie's silent life. I thought of Mr. Miller and that last handful of earth, and I let the pages slip from my fingers.

La Gatita

SHE REMINDED ME of a cat, the way it brushes against you as if by accident, hoping to draw all of your attention. Her eyes were black, wide open, unblinking it seemed, and they sought mine at every moment. I was suddenly nervous and tried to stop myself from staring into them as I talked to the guy standing with her. She hung on his arm, resting her head on his shoulder from time to time, but kept staring directly at me, moving her chin up, then down, turning her pale face slowly in quarters. But the eyes never wavered.

They had been loitering on the sidewalk in front of the hotel, much like the ubiquitous hippie street vendors with their little blankets covered with pretty rocks on strings. But what these two were selling wasn't readily apparent. They both spoke decent English, much better than my Spanish, I thought. The man kept talking to me about tourist sites in Peru, but I was clearly not interested in them, and I got the feeling he couldn't give a damn about explaining them to me anyway. We were all pretending. Every time he thought of a new subject, he'd brighten and say, "Hey," and then poke me in the stomach through my T-shirt. It was irritating me. I wondered why I kept loitering there at the curb. But then each time I looked at her, I looked a bit longer. It didn't take long for me to understand she wasn't affectionate with him exactly, just comfortable. With an exaggerated sweeping gesture, he brushed my stomach with the back of his hand. I began to suspect I was being hit on.

He had spoken to me first, introducing himself as I broke a cardinal traveler's rule and stood in the middle of the street looking at a tourist map. I only needed to take out everything from my money belt and count it right there in front of God and everybody to make my idiocy complete. He introduced the girl as Marcela, and she stepped in close to me, slowly, as if choreographed and rehearsed, and kissed my cheek close to my mouth, lush soft lips, slightly parted, and then lingered there breathfully before backing away. I was lingering myself. I suddenly felt too tired to walk away.

Another guest at the hotel, a young Austrian man with long, blond hair in a ponytail, approached from across the street and greeted these two Peruvians as if they were old friends, though, like me, he had probably only been in town a day or two. He promised to return later but had to be somewhere and needed to get something from his room. Chao.

The man turned back to me, poked my stomach, "He is a nice person. From Australia. Hey, have you seen the Gold Museum here in Lima? Hm?"

A taxi driver slowed down, honked, and gestured to me with a frown as though he had been waiting for me and I had finally shown up. "Do you need a ride or what?" I shook my head at him and he drove off annoyed. The man continued. "...Hey, do you like to eat *ceviche*? There is a wonderful place for *ceviche* just on the other side of the Plaza de Armas. If you want, I can take you there... The conquistador Francisco Pizarro created this plaza. Do you know? Los conquistadores?"

One of their hippie friends stood up from his blanket of shells and paperclip jewelry and gave Marcela a wide, loose belt of beads. She fastened it around her narrow waist and raised her slight wrists over her head and shook like a belly dancer to rattle them. I couldn't really hear what her chatty partner was saying, but I sensed a drop in his level of enthusiasm as he knew I wasn't listening. But he continued, "Hey, have you been to...? Hey, another thing you must see is..."

"It would look good on you," she said. She took the bead belt off and stepped up against me. I tensed. She wrapped her arms behind me and looped the belt around, pulling me close. I could smell her hair, the vague fragrance of the generic fruits of soap products. She fastened the buckle. "Mm. There. Dance."

"I don't think so."

She bumped her hip against my thigh to encourage me but then removed the belt as she pressed against me, coyly disappointed in my nonperformance.

She stared at me again. Her black hair, in straight lines to the corner of her jaw, created a Gothic frame for a picture of seduction. She suggested we meet somewhere. I hesitated at the vague "we" and cast a glance at the talker who was looking off down the street, unconcerned, but suddenly far away -- though not far enough. She appeared very young. Bad idea. I made an animal decision, not a reasonable one. "OK."

"At six?"

I looked at my watch. "No. 6:30."

"Here on this corner?" she asked. She bit a pink lip that turned white along her fine teeth. Lolita. The clear skin, the lips parted, chin forward, eyes penetrating.

"In the café?"

She turned slowly to look where I pointed. "Mm. Can't afford to drink there."

I shrugged, suspecting the popular trick of finagling drinks out of tourists. Like the infamous Mojito Scam of Cuba: oh, first day here? Let me show you where Hemingway used to drink, and I'll order a double round of his mojitos, and then you will pick up the inflated tab because I have no money when the bill comes and the bouncer is big and you are a foreigner and afraid to say no. Different countries, same routine.

"OK, then, the corner. 6:30."

A slow, dreamy smile spread over her face as she nodded, still biting her lip. It was too much. I started to wonder if she had a bag of glue in her back pocket.

We parted. She kissed my cheek again, brushed my elbow with her fingertips. The man shook my hand tenderly, "And don't forget, my name is Jorge." He patted his chest. I pinched my lips into some semblance of a smile.

I stepped back into the hotel, a rough-around-the-edges building from a better time that had likely been converted from offices and apartments to cheap accommodations with high ceilings and fancy crown molding, the paint flaking off. Shoestring travel comes with its own exhausting price, exacted in shoe leather, patience, and bed bugs. Saving a taxi fare for a two-mile walk through a gauntlet of hawkers, squeezing in with a hundred people on a fifty-person chicken bus, going door-to-door some evenings like a backpacking Mary and Joseph – "Is there a cheap room in the inn?"

It was a tradeoff, but one I was willing to make. The typical traveler ended up running from site to site, breathless and photo bombing an exotic life for a week or two to impress the poor bastards stuck back at the office. That wasn't for me. I didn't take vacations; I just quit jobs. Then I traveled light and with no particular itinerary until an empty bank account sent me back for another round of paychecks.

The people I met by lingering longer were both the reward and the curse. One day you might find a Maya holy man willing to talk about his mystical world over a beer in a Guatemalan bar; the next day it's some fellow expat who latches on to you at the bus station and thinks you are both part of some sacred Brotherhood of the Common Passport, obliged to walk among the strange streets of strange lands and condemn them for their tainted tap water. Sorting out the good souls from those who just want to get into your pocket, your head, or your pants eventually gets tiresome.

Sometimes I wondered why I was doing it. When locals or fellow travelers asked me why I came to Peru, I was hard pressed for an answer. "To see Machu Picchu," I'd say if I didn't really give a damn. "It's been my dream since I first saw it in a magazine when I was a kid. There's something so... so... *spiritual* about the place, don't you think?" They rarely sensed the irony.

I WAS BACK in the street at 6:30, still obeying some cultural imperative of punctuality, which much of the world—at the very least Lima, Peru—didn't seem to know anything about. I waited only a short while, telling myself it was best to avoid this girl—certainly too young and guaranteed trouble. I had the strange sense my resolve was being tested. No one was looking. I was a thirty-odd-year-old zoo animal that wakes one day to find the cage wide open.

I knew this scenario. I had seen it before—middle-aged men or older from North America lurking around big cities in Latin America, picking up young girls, often underage. Something they would never think to do back home. It was as if by stepping outside national borders they were somehow outside moral limits as well.

Back in Panama City, I remembered fat, white gringos sprawled in sidewalk cafes as if beached there by a rogue wave, sipping beer with ice in it, wiping the sweating glasses across foreheads that appeared to have been rubbed completely with rouge. Young innocence perched on their knees, awaiting the next round of drinks and the next promenade through the shops where they'd be treated to a few "gifts." I had always thought the word "gringo" a sort of harmless joke until I saw these men -- ex-military or Canal Zone men, or portly pensioners with real-estate incomes back home -- chewing on cigars, patting youthful bottoms, and talking too loudly about how the whole place could be improved, how stupid the locals were. They were parodies of themselves, and they knew no limits. From then on I never wanted to be called "gringo." In places like that, the locals spit the word.

I checked my watch: 6:50. From around the corner came the blaring horns of a marching band, brassy and bold in the style of a funeral march in New Orleans, but lacking the soul. I peered around the edge of the building, and at the end of the street was a religious parade. Holy Week was approaching more quickly than this procession. A group of perhaps twenty-five men were carrying a mammoth platform adorned in gold and lace and featuring a statue of the Virgin beneath an ornate canopy. The bearers leaned into the weight of it, walking at an angle to the ground. One side pushed as the other side swayed away slightly and up a bit. Then with the heavy movement of ocean surge, it would sweep back again. And with each sway, with solemn faces, they all took a mere fraction of a step forward. This pendulum sort of motion perhaps eases the labor – or exacerbates it; the greater the suffering, the greater the reward.

At the opposite end of the street was their destination, San Francisco Monastery, a bright yellow colonial affair, complete with catacombs. Deep beneath the street, the anonymous dead of the last centuries had been reduced to a collection of dusky skulls arranged in concentric circles at the bottom of what looked like a wide well. A dim yellow light lit the shallow cavern so that all could see the macabre final communion; the worn teeth sank into the dust, taking one last bite in unison. Upstairs, heavy in gold and painted gore, the promise of eternity outlived its servants below. Out in the street, the men struggled to get here with the burden on their shoulders.

I stood in the middle of the street before the swaying Virgin and decided it might make a good photo. I ran inside the hotel for my camera and returned to take a few shots before the light faded completely. As I went to one knee in the middle of the street to get a better angle, someone called my name. I ignored it and kept focusing. Again, I heard my name. I turned and there he was—what was his name again? Jorge.

He asked me if I liked processions. I stood up and stared at him. He patted my stomach with the back of his hand. "Hey, are you going to be here for Semana Santa?"

"No."

"There are many processions for that week."

"Interesting."

"Do you like the clothes the women are wearing?"

I sighed. "Sure."

"It is traditional."

"I imagine."

"Are you hungry?"

"Not particularly."

His smile faltered, and then he looked around as though searching for another subject of conversation. He found one. "Hey, have you been to the Museum of Art?"

I hadn't. "Yes, I went yesterday."

"Oh... So tell me about your country."

I wanted to get away, but I could not figure out how to do that without him following. I wondered where his little catlike friend had strayed. "What do you want to know?"

"Oh, I don't know. Is it like here?"

"Not so much. Well, I mean it is and it isn't. Like any place in the world. People are people. But then there are things that are wildly different."

"Wildly?" he raised one eyebrow.

"Er..." I looked away quickly. "Well, this procession. Or ceviche."

"Oh, you like *ceviche*?"

I loved it. "Not really."

"The *ceviche* here is the best in the world."

"I've heard that."

"Hey, do you like—"

"Hey, listen, I'm feeling a little tired. I guess I'll just go back to the hotel. Long bus ride back from Cusco, you know? Maybe I'll see you later..." And I was gone.

I STOOD IN the balcony of my hotel room watching the people pass below. The balconies of Lima are tourist attractions in their own right. Ornately carved, they are diverse works of art as much as private perches overlooking the streets. A person could do a photo gallery of them all, a coffee-table book for the people who keep coffee tables but not balconies. I leaned on my elbows, an emperor observing his people. I was bored and debated wandering around in the streets, but I knew I would be searching, not wandering. I heard the call of a cat somewhere. I scanned the sidewalks, the rooftops across the way. No sign of it.

When I looked back to the street, she had just rounded the corner and was passing beneath my perch. I meowed down to her, and she looked up.

"Why are you up there?"

"So I can see down your shirt."

"I don't understand."

"Nothing. Just watching people."

"You will come down?"

"I'm thinking about it."

Even from that distance the black eyes drilled me.

"Where were you at 6:30?"

"I was there," I pointed to the corner behind her, "waiting for you."

"I didn't see you."

"Big corner."

"I don't understand."

"Not important. I'm coming down."

I swung open the heavy wooden door in the lobby and stepped out into the street. After 11 p.m., the outer iron gate, which now stood open, would be padlocked shut, and only the hotel night clerk had the key to open it. The hotel suddenly appeared to me like some sort of safe house or an embassy in a hostile land.

She kissed me in greeting, and I shivered. We were alone. The street at the moment was empty. "What will we do?" she asked with a coy upward tilt to her chin, her face so close that I had to look back and forth between her eyes.

Before I could answer, someone called my name. I probably should have thanked him, but a darker part of me scowled from behind a fake smile as he came around the corner.

"So you have rested?"

"Not really. I'm going to the store to get a bottle of something to wash down a pill."

I even pulled out a serendipitous Tylenol that was lodged in my pocket among strange coins and lint and held it forth in my open palm. We all looked at it uncertainly.

"Maybe we can meet later tonight," he offered.

"Yes, maybe."

She said nothing as I left them, and I felt her watching me as I crossed the street to a small convenience store.

I bought a bottle of neon-yellow Inka Kola and threw the pill and its coating of lint into the cardboard box full of wrappers and empties on the floor in front of the counter. I drank half of the bottle quickly, waited a moment, and then stuck my head back into the street. Empty. I headed off in the opposite direction, hoping to make the corner before someone called my name. The streets looked harmless enough, but the other guests at the hotel and even some of the hotel workers warned me about them after dark.

Streetlights had come on, and many of the shops were already closed. I passed a cantina spilling its mossy warmth and a couple of staggering clientele onto the walk. I eyed a group of children playing with something in a doorway across the street.

"Do you know what piranhas are?" someone had asked me in the hotel lobby, a German guy traveling after living in Peru for six months with some kind of internship in economics.

"Sure. The fish?"

"No, no. Street kids. Gangs of them. Maybe seven, maybe eight years old. Little kids. They come along, and there are maybe twenty of them or maybe thirty, and they surround you, and they take everything. Money, backpack, keys, jacket—all your clothes sometimes."

"Clothes?"

"They leave you naked. It's better than if they cut you. Sometimes they do that. Very dangerous. Be careful at night."

I didn't believe him. Or at least exaggeration had taken its monster share of the story. Perhaps they weren't his embellishments, just the cumulative edits of the travelers' network's imagination. But the truest part of the story was the fear. If something bad happens in a place, the network instantly knows and spreads it like gospel. A single attack on a tourist can tarnish a place's reputation for months or even years.

I found a man with a food cart and ate some *salchipapas*, essentially hot dog pieces and French fries. I wandered another hour or so before making my way over to the Plaza de Armas. The large brass fountain in the center was shut off. Even the water wasn't venturing out in the dark. A dozen palm trees stood among the few patches of grass separated from the paving stones by low-hanging chains. I found a vacant bench and watched a few people meander past. Some were travelers; others looked more like the trinket hippies out in front of the hotel. I saw a couple of police officers wandering along the perimeter and wondered vaguely if they weren't more dangerous than most of the other people I might be wary of here.

A small voice came from behind me. "You are very fast."

I looked over my shoulder and saw her figure turned silhouette in the glare of a street lamp beyond. She could see my face, but hers was a dark space.

Had she been following me? I held up the empty soda bottle. "Caffeine."

She didn't understand, but nodded. She turned the grassy corner, and her face reappeared. She stood in front of me, her midriff bare, her pierced navel at the level of my face. Her pant legs brushed against mine as she seemed to be about to straddle my crossed legs. She hitched her hands in her back pockets and thrust her hips forward slightly so that the bones rose beneath the smooth skin just above her belt. I searched the park and could not see her friend anywhere.

"Why are you out here alone?"

I shrugged. "Couldn't sleep."

She bit her lip once again and fixed me with an eye. The hair swung out from the side of her face as she tilted her head. "Do you have trouble sleeping?" she asked in almost a whisper.

I didn't answer, just looked back at her to see how long she would stare. Long. I looked away and uncrossed my legs, bumping one of hers. "Sorry."

"Not important," she told me. She lined up her shoes touching the tips to the ends of my own and then looked up at me again.

"Marcela," I said to no one.

"Yes?"

"I like the name... M, like the sound you make when food is delicious... The C—or is it an S?—like a sigh."

"A sigh?"

"Er, *un suspiro*."

"Oh."

"And the L, with the tongue, very sensual, the mouth curves around it."

She smiled stiffly. "That is nice."

"Beautiful. Appropriate name."

Her body tensed like a small animal's does when something unexpected enters the field it thought empty and safe. Some of the seduction shifted from her face when the expression froze, and something pitiable took its place. I could feel the sexiness blow away like the scattering trash, and as if on cue, something light and plastic skittered in the gutter.

I fell silent. Somehow I had broken protocol. As though I had misspoken the dialogue and the play had fallen out of its exchange, and neither actor could find a place to resume. She crossed her arms, and her head leaned to the other side; she stared off back toward the park.

She was a child, naked in a dirty street. I cringed and sought my next words in the tops of my shoes where they still lined up with hers.

"How old are you, Marcela?"

She looked at me once again but with the subtle friction of defiance, as though I was scolding her with my question. "Guess," she told me.

I never could, especially in Latin America where youth seemed to live longer in the cheeks and smiles of many of their older women, or else age came suddenly, making even teenagers look as though they had seen decades of life's blunt edge. The best bet was the eyes sometimes. "Nineteen?"

It was only the second smile I had seen from her, not counting the concealing one of a moment before. "No. Sixteen."

I stole her concealing smile for myself. "Nice," I managed to say. "Out kind of late, aren't you?"

She sat down next to me, but not so close. We were now adult and child.

"I am always out this late."

I was going to ask about parents but stopped myself.

"Um, where do you live?"

She jerked her head toward the opposite side of the park. "In an apartment. There are rooms there. Jorge lives there too. We are five."

"I see. You have family?"

She darted a look at me. "Yes. But I can't live there anymore."

She stated that with closure so I did not ask more. She stared down at her feet, her hands on either side of her clutching the edge of the bench. Her hair hung limply, obscuring my view of her profile until she pulled it behind her ear.

"I leave tomorrow. I return to my country."

"Yes?" She looked up with some interest. "Is it nice there?"

"Yes, sometimes. But I often get bored."

"Me, too."

I didn't know where to go with the conversation. I couldn't ask her about traveling. It was enough to be so young, but even the older people around her rarely had the resources to go anywhere. I felt uncomfortable with my freedom, my opportunities, my lack of firm boundaries. The imagined edge that I was living on—not owning a car or house, no health insurance or significant savings—didn't change the fact that I was from a land of plenty, far beyond her hardest efforts.

"You have been to many places?"

Modesty urged me to say no, but respect compelled me to nod.

"Where was your favorite?"

I looked in her eyes, trying to imagine that only moments ago they had stirred something dark and disturbing in me. Now I felt protective.

"Here, actually. Peru."

"Really?" She wrinkled her nose with surprise and perhaps a little suspicion.

"Yes, for certain. It is a beautiful land. Lima. Cusco. Lake Titicaca. Machu Picchu, of course. So much culture. You're lucky to live here."

She shrugged. "Maybe. But I want to leave."

"Where would you go?"

"I don't know. Maybe the United States. That is your country?"

"Yes. Why there?"

"Everyone says it is nice. There is money there."

I wanted to tell her there was so much more in life than money, but again it is a luxury to be able to say such a thing. Maybe it isn't even true.

I looked at my watch. "Damn. My flight leaves early. I'd better go back to my hotel."

She nodded with a polite smile.

We both stood up, and she stood close enough that I could have taken her gently in my arms. "Well, take care of yourself, Marcela..."

"Yes, you also."

I kissed her forehead and left her in the park. Lines would not be crossed. Our limits define us, for better and for worse. While I wander this earth, alien to my own culture and a stranger in the next, I am sometimes not sure who I am. But I am damned sure who I am not.

I didn't want to be mean to Jorge. He seemed nice enough, but he was dull. Hell, I was dull at the moment, my edges worn away by the road. What on earth kept him from boredom? It made me wonder how many times I had persisted too long with someone—attraction perhaps glossing over the glaringly insipid reality of our exchange—or how often I had misread mere conversational interest as something more.

I had returned to the convenience store across from my hotel, which was still open at almost midnight. I sat at a plastic patio table drinking a bottle of mango juice and watching the large raggedy woman who ran the place gradually rest her chin on her ample bosom under the blaring television mounted in the corner. Jorge found me there sitting opposite an empty chair. I didn't invite him, but he sat anyway, grinning like it was some grand coincidence that we encountered each other there after all this time.

"Hey, the procession was beautiful wasn't it? Do you like the festivities? All the flowers..."

What was my answer? I thought.

"... I have been to the United States. Have you ever been to Los Angeles or San Francisco?"

I crossed my legs, then uncrossed them. He was just toying with me, a sort of cosmic justice for any uninvited interests I had displayed for various women in the past. Was I ever this persistent? The poking, the measured touches continued. No matter how wide the table was or how far I leaned back, somehow he was still able to brush my arm with his fingertips.

I took the offensive, hoping to actively bore him. "So your little friend... Marcela..."

83

The corners of his smile tightened. "Yes?"

"How old is she?"

"How old did she say?"

"Sixteen."

"They say sixteen, then it's fifteen... or fourteen."

"I think she could lie better than sixteen."

He just waved me away, and I saw him glance up at the television.

"So, er... Jorge, what do you do?"

"I was a student."

"And what did you study?"

"Nothing interesting. Business."

"You seem a little old for a student."

"Only twenty-five."

"Or twenty-six or twenty-seven, right?" I reached out and jabbed his shoulder a couple times and winked. He smiled weakly. "So that makes la gatita a little young for you, no?"

"Little cat? I don't understand."

"I mean, Marcela."

His eyes narrowed at me. "What makes you think she interests me like that?"

"No reason. She reminds me of my girlfriend. Back home." Neither existed.

He looked tired. "Oh yes?" His gaze flicked to the TV for a second.

"Very much. Something in the eyes. Yes, the eyes."

"So young as well?" he asked ironically.

"Well not fourteen or fifteen certainly... So Jorge, what do you do now?"

"I work. At a store. I sell clothes." He glanced at the television again, a bit longer.

"Fascinating."

The woman behind the counter awoke with a snort and looked around, wiping her mouth self-consciously. Like a reflex she asked, "What would you like?"

I stood up and went to the counter, "Another bottle of mango juice."

Behind me Jorge said, "And a beer." I ignored him.

She came back from the fridge with both and set them on the glass counter. I laid out exact change for the juice and stepped away pretending to watch the television as I drank. Jorge seemed uncomfortable. The woman looked back and forth between us and held up the beer. "You want beer?" she asked him. He shook his head. The woman rolled her eyes and turned toward the fridge with the bottle.

"Wait. Here." I dropped a few more coins on the glass, and they rattled to a stop.

He looked back at the TV as I set the bottle on the table. "Oh, thank you." He took a large swallow. "You are nice."

"No, I'm not. But that's not important." I remained standing. "Jorge, it's been a pleasure." I squeezed his hand, wet with the condensation from his drink. "But I need to sleep. Early flight."

"Have a safe trip."

"It's already over, but thanks."

I stepped back into the street where a couple of stray dogs picked at some trash along the sidewalk. They cleared away, skittish, walking sideways as I passed. I felt imposing and fearsome. I pressed the hotel buzzer and waited, while down

85

the block, a street light flickered and went dark. All the shop windows had metal doors pulled down tightly over them, as if bracing for a storm that never comes. Colonial yellow had become dusky gray, and the city took on the sullen gloom of an abandoned amusement park. After a couple of moments, the door opened, and without speaking a word, an old, withered man turned a key in the large brass padlock to open the gate. I slipped past him as the iron bars clanged shut, and he rattled the lock back into place. I crossed the lobby without looking back, and as I started up the stairs, I felt the thud resonate through the building as the heavy wooden door closed behind me.

Mosaic

A MAN WALKS INTO Antioch. Now it is Antakya, now that the Turks have it. Constantinople is Istanbul, Sancta Sophia is Ayasofya. But we'll call it Antioch, to retain its churchgoer's familiarity. Something started here. With all the pomp and circumstance, and Gothic, Baroque, gilded, flying-buttressed cathedrals, it seems ironic that the first church of St. Peter was just a humble hole in the side of a nearby hill. Or perhaps the cathedrals are what are ironic.

Now Antioch is a borderland; Arab and Turk mix and mingle. A vague space. A perfect limbo. A man finds a cheap hotel and collapses, fully clothed, on a bed. The drawn-out cry of the muezzin chases him to uncertain sleep in the gray light of dusk.

The man tries to draw a bubble around himself, a sense of being from a sense of place. There are limits to redefine.

He wakes up in a bed that reeks vaguely of sweat. Cobwebs in his eyes and the corners of the room, and the bed is one giant rusted spring, broken and defeated beneath him. Coins, crumpled bills, and a battered passport on a nightstand refashioned from a vegetable crate. The Turk at the front desk watches him with no expression as he shuffles through the lobby into the street. He has been ill, and the sunlight of late afternoon surprises him. He has no watch.

At a corner shop he orders a sandwich of lamb, thinly sliced from the vertical spit in the front window, where fat and juices bleed from the mass shaped like the meaty thigh of a giant. Two bites and he feels nausea expand like a balloon in his gut. Uludağ soda then; just some sugar at least. How long does it take to starve? How little to sustain? He leaves limp, soiled lira bills, denominations nearly obliterated.

He sees a Muslim man washing his feet in a public fountain and so wonders what day it is. Perhaps Friday. At the street corner a vendor speaks to him from the back of the throat. But he knows no Arabic. Only no. *La'*. The vendor blinks, then switches to Turkish. The vendor is asking for the time, and he wonders the same. *Bilmiyorum*, he says, I don't know, holding up his naked wrist, and counters, What day is it? The vendor is confused. After a pause the vendor says, *Cuma*. Friday.

Night falls fast in uncertain hour like sleep, and he is still in the streets nibbling at a pack of stale crackers, swallowing their dust in place of a meal. He sits on a low stone wall, watches the street. Two veiled women pass and look at him with guarded expressions, possibly some apprehension. His skin is pale, even ghostly in the edges of a streetlight's gloom. Only the motion of his eyes assures them he is among the living.

Thunder shakes cobblestones, and in strobe-like interludes, house fronts appear and disappear in the dark. He hadn't noticed that the black sky had swallowed up the stars. He steps under an awning, defending himself from the sudden anger of the rain. It only lasts fifteen minutes. But when it is done, a shimmering layer coats the road and rolls tiny pebbles down the hillside. So he climbs.

Below him Antioch. Nothing profound. No epiphany. No saints. Just red-tiled rooftops that are now gray-tiled rooftops and sulking in shadows between meager lights. He swallows another papery piece of cracker and gags. All his efforts of the hour before are lost and mingle with the rain, tumbling with pebbles down the mountainside.

An old Turkish woman finds him propped up against the stoop of her front door and half carries him inside. Someone else's legs are propelling his torso, and he is grateful.

She brings him yogurt, and his whole being clenches at the thought; but she insists. It is a cold soup. He sips at it, sour on his tongue, bits of cucumber, soft, simple to chew like baby food. He sleeps.

HE SEES HER for the first time, only months after arriving in Istanbul, in a smoky club near Taksim, a cavern below the street where his fellow expatriates have taken him. She holds him boldly with her eyes, black as the kohl she's drawn them with, and he looks away. She takes him to the dance floor and, with every touch and smile, he bends deeper to her beckoning. They speak of nothing, merely names, titles, and trivial facts. He has pretexts of work for being here, caught between two continents, but the truth is he is drifting and searching for safety in an intimacy that never comes, a seedling skittering across the surface of the hard, dry earth. He sees warmth in her but like a reflection of moonlight on dark waters. She sees him for his vulnerability and shifts within her skin; her sex opens to him. He will fall here amid the trappings of Byzantium buried beneath cracking pavement, under the sharp shadows of stern mosques and the weight of the timeless sea that lingers on the breeze off the Bosphorus.

WHAT DAY IS IT? he asks. Sunday, the old woman replies. Which Sunday? She doesn't answer but goes into the kitchen for more of the yogurt soup. He manages to prop himself up on an elbow. He is ragged and his hair feels like broom bristles planted painfully in his scalp. He musses it with his fingers in hopes of making the stiffness go away.

He untangles more lira bills from his pocket but she pushes his hand away, shaking her head vigorously. He leaves through the door backward, bowing and stammering through gratitudes.

He finds himself in a museum full of mosaics. Roman gods. Neptune and his trident, a fish twists its tail above his shoulder, a minion and its god. But who decided this was a god? He sees divinity imposed on a mere fisherman, on simple flecks of color. The chips of stone swell and magnify, and the image is lost to him; he lost in it. The spaces between absorb his sight and the picture becomes empty space, something inchoate, a plane of potential, waiting to call a god into being. To summon forth a god.

He steps into a patio, looking up through small trees at the sun. When he looks down, he realizes he has stepped over a low-hanging chain and is himself part of a large mosaic laid out across the floor. The pale chips of brown and beige support him above the abyss. He steps quickly back over the chain and looks to see if he has been observed. There is something unsettling for him here. Some of the mosaics are missing portions, like old puzzles forgotten in the closet for years and put together again as far as they'll go, for the sake of remembering what it was to create.

He is running down the street. Something only young delivery boys do, perhaps with tea services delicately balanced. He runs to nowhere until exhaustion. Then, pausing to understand where he is, he turns toward where he thinks his hotel lies.

WHERE DID ALL of this really begin? Here in Antioch? Damascus? Or before that, all the way back in Istanbul? Something that grew inside him, rising in his chest, a desire or a need that shortened his breath. Where does this experience begin? What is the first piece?

IN SYRIA, the woman. The mystery of a veil, the temptation of what is hidden. Her willingness moves him forward, and he tries to let something out, something vile, an aimless vengeance. He fails to go through with it. He sends her away with easy money. Hours later he awakens to frightening illness feeling like the life is pouring out of him. In the morning he tries to hitchhike back to the relative familiarity of Turkey. He rides in the back of a truck full of produce. Cabbages like thick skulls from some horrible massacre, and he is carted away with the corpses.

THE CALL TO PRAYER penetrates his skull and tears him from deep sleep. He lies there, suddenly aware, his breath shallow and fast, his skin rippled in a cold sweat. The same hotel, broken bed, the overturned vegetable crate near his head. How many days? He threads through his pockets, collecting the wrinkled lira bills in a pile before his face on the bed. They shiver almost imperceptibly with his shallow breath.

Just down the street, he walks into a barber shop with mud in its gutters, and the man wordlessly shows him to a chair. The entire exchange, in fact, is without words, only gestures for beard, for shave. A hot towel covers his face, encloses his nose, and he breathes deeply of its humidity of dark, earthy caverns. He remembers the prostitute, closes his eyes. The blade is cold against his throat but fast. He opens one eye to look at himself in the mirror. A nick blossoms a drop of scarlet, and the barber wipes it away embarrassed, quickly dabs it with a styptic pencil. The cologne burns, and he welcomes the contrast to the leaden discomfort of nausea, the fatigue of his insides.

IN A PASSAGEWAY in a *souk* in Damascus, a woman is waiting. She pulls a veil across her face but never takes her eyes from him. The fabric pulses with her quick breath like an artery below the surface of the skin. The market is close, a honeycomb maze of dim chambers and corridors, loud, stinking of freshly slaughtered animals, dust, and human smells that attack the senses. But he skirts the edge where the activity begins and ends and the shadows enclose and reveal in secret. He leans against the wall, hot and dirty. She touches his cheek with a moist hand.

THE CALL TO PRAYER accuses him, an infidel in his bed.

"WHERE IS THE next town?"

The question makes no sense. He receives a blank but patient stare, so he gives up and walks past the front desk to the street. He makes his way to the center of Antioch until he arrives at a river that sags in the earth, low and humiliated, dark with poisons and filth. He looks down off the bridge and sees his blurred reflection undulating over a surface of milky coffee. He is thinner. He cannot see his eyes; he reaches up to his face to test the reflection. His eyes. He touches them like strange discoveries taken from deep within his pockets.

He remembers the mosaic of Neptune. Were there eyes or only empty spaces, missing pieces? A kingdom dark, never coming up for air. Reigning but without the warmth of the sun. A mere consolation, a substitute for the real. Descent. Depths. Abysmal. From a Peter Gabriel song he remembers, *Dancing for the slow release, first the boy and then the beast...*

ISTANBUL TURNS FROM his kingdom to his wasteland. He is powerless and suddenly a stranger. He finds where she disappeared to, the apartment she moved into. She refuses to open the door, doesn't answer her phone. He stands in the street, the rain of spring still runs cold like winter's blood making him shudder uncontrollably. Her window high above holds forth the charcoal sky, but he is convinced he sees her face lurking beneath the reflection, a drowning victim forever lost.

He clings to a lamppost and feels the weight of a deluge like a verdict.

HE RETURNS TO the museum and takes a seat before Neptune. He stares at the puzzle. Each piece meaningless by itself, each memory an empty clue, isolated. The body disappears from the waist down, lost in the murky gray where the missing chips are replaced by patches of plaster which become the rising waters of forgetting. He tries to imagine what existed before. What had first been remembered from that gray void? Who had brought it forth and to what end? Not long after, it was forgotten, buried or abandoned, and now remembered once again, a mysterious visitor, nevertheless familiar. He stands to leave the museum, hesitates at the direction of the exit. Using the sun in the courtyard and his idea of the time, he can find north, but what does it matter?

HE ENTERS A MOSQUE in Damascus wherein lies the tomb of John the Baptist. He has seen the misplaced forearm of the Baptist in a museum back in Istanbul. The Baptist had also been detached from his head--or detached from his body. What lies in the tomb? He wanders lonely in the late afternoon, drunk with his immersion in the other, somehow feeling released from the confines of his Western conscience and compelled to forget his sensitivity. He is rude to beggars and doesn't care. He stares openly at the veiled women who come and go in the open markets and is surprised to find a pair of eyes that do not turn away. They invite. He follows.

OUTSIDE ANTIOCH LIE the crumbling ramparts of forgotten kings and crusades. The rocks themselves seem to melt and flow back to the earth. Beneath his shirt, his ribs continue their patient rise to his skin.

There is a church here somewhere. A hole in the side of a hill. Another empty space that defines. Just as the spaces in Neptune back at the museum define and limit a god. He goes to seek that space, walking through narrow streets, rising gradually toward the hills. What is it to be invincible? Or simply to be?

He falls to the cobblestones. The sun is strong; the light burns his eyelids until the color of the world is red. He opens them then, and all the world is faded like aging paint. An old woman's eyes accuse him, and so he rights himself to appear purposeful in his place on the ground. Only stopping to rest in the sunshine. But he sits like a broken prophet among the stones of the road.

SHE LAUGHS without reservation, openly in the streets, drawing nervous looks. He finds it powerful, entrancing. There is a wild look that sometimes enters her eyes. When they kiss, she bites his lower lip and pulls, not always gently. She has little money but she somehow manages. She moves in with him for several weeks and he walks confidently to the school each morning. She is something he never had. She is woman, mother earth drawing him inside her, where he thinks he is created but in fact she consumes him. He sees divinity in clay, and she despises him for his weakness. He sleeps unaware, an innocent who only thinks in terms of love. The minarets rise above Istanbul like sentries guarding his exotic new home. He returns home every day to find her staring from the balcony over the narrow street, a meal growing cold on the kitchen table. But weeks later, she is not there above him, and he climbs the steps two at a time to find her curled in bed where she had been when he had awakened behind her in the morning, her back curved like defensive ramparts.

They eat the meal in silence, and she laughs raucously when a bit of food drops from his fork to his lap. He smiles weakly, and she laughs even harder. She stares at him through the rest of the meal. He takes the dishes to the sink and begins washing them. She stands beside him, musses his hair, takes his earlobe between her teeth and bites hard. He shoves her away angrily, holds the tender ear. Something of a sneer is nestled into her smile. She scowls and lets out a short shrill scream through her parted teeth and then laughs as one tired or drunk. She leaves him in the kitchen holding a plate with soapsuds slipping to the floor.

The next day she is gone.

IN THE MIDDLE of a Syrian night, he awakens immediate with adrenaline. His mouth fills with saliva; he knows he must move quickly. He slips on his shoes and rushes down the hall leaving the door wide open, unconcerned at the moment for his belongings. In the bathroom he collapses, hanging his head over the edge of a rusted bathtub. He vomits violently, his whole body contracting with the effort. He soils himself as well and feels his will being drawn from him. Beads of sweat begin to sting his eyes, and he shivers with the cold of the steel tub against his neck. His vision becomes a fuzzy red at the edges and begins closing toward the center to shut him off from the horror of the moment. He fights to focus his sight on the mess before him in the tub. Eventually the tremors of his body subside, and he is left breathing shallowly, his pulse a weak twitch in his flesh. After an hour, he pulls himself up and uses a bucket in the corner to try to clean up the small space. He stumbles back to the room and drifts into nightmares of a dark, sweating passageway like the throat of a dying beast.

WHAT HAND SORTED senseless chips to make meaning? No one would ever suggest it was chance. Not even Turks and their love of kismet. Lost in thought he pauses outside a holy refuge. An old man emerges from the cave church. The light that falls inside illuminates one small place on the soil; the rest remains submerged in darkness but exists as much as anything else. It is not the rock that holds meaning: the empty space is the reality. A different hour, a different world. A different earth. The old man stands before him, frowning.

You are a stranger here, *efendim.*

I wanted that.

You are not afraid?

I was afraid when I was not a stranger but felt like one.

What did you come here for?

To try things. To find things.

The old man snorts. Yourself, right?

No. I came to lose that. Obliterate it.

You can never do that. Something always takes its place. Like the pharaohs.

I have never been to Egypt.

The statues there. All the same. Scratch out a title and scratch in another. It makes no difference.

Were you born here?

No. I live here.

Why?

The old man shrugs. It chose me.

I don't think so. People choose.

You don't understand. That's why you are sick.

I am sick for what I ate. Or something that bit me.

You need a doctor.

Yes.

Don't look here. Go to the capital.

HE FEELS USED, controlled. He is narrated into that dark passageway deep in the souk by a blind lust that might rise up in anyone, the animal urge that drives and consumes. Just as life consumes life, thrives on the death of the next being, lust exhausts and devours, consumes the passion until the peace settles in, the temporary bliss of desirelessness. Isn't this what the portly Buddha spoke of in another land? No, this is an artificial nirvana that will call again to be fed. Only to deny itself.

The scratch of fabric against the back of his hand, burying itself in the folds, searching. A gasp from under a veil. His shame is in plain view. The smell of jasmine intoxicates him, and he sighs in dismay, takes her hand, and pulls her along the dim tunnel as though they were pursued.

HE LEAVES HIS postcards on the battered vegetable crate. Outdated photos of various sites from a different country and empty white space behind them. Ticket stubs from buses. Several coins of almost no value. A few broken capsules of a stomach medicine scatter powder across peeling paint. Clues for the archaeologists, he thinks. The rest of his belongings tumble in disorder into his dirty knapsack.

He steps out into the sun and pauses to look at the streets. Antioch fell. Just as Rome fell or Greece. Or Poseidon to Neptune. But in falling, none of them ceases to exist. They are only altered in evanescent labels and judgements. Colors and weight made lighter by history.

He purchases a ticket. He asks the clerk a question then checks the clock. He has ten minutes. Time returns. A moment is defined and will end.

The bus is a long common casket of cold steel, the passengers laid out in their seats for a journey through the night. It is directed and strong. The engine spouts diesel into the parking lot. A destination. Ankara, the capital. He carries his knapsack with him, stores it in the compartment above his head. Then he sits in the last seat in back and leans his head against the tinted glass, watching the activity outside. As the bus departs, an old man throws a coffee cup full of water across its back for its safe return. Tradition is habit; superstition its justification.

He closes his eyes to sleep and ceases to exist.

Maple Seeds

I ARRIVE EARLY to find their house quiet and empty. I'm always early it seems, anxious to go somewhere, be somewhere. And they are typically running behind. Couples have inertia, and it can be difficult to get them in motion or alter their direction. So I sit to wait for my friends on the cool stones of their front steps, which, along with the yard, are littered with lime-green maple seeds that are helicoptering down around me in the midday breeze.

The shaded yard is fragrant with cut grass, pine sap, and the mossy air from the low, damp spots along the walk. The buzz of a distant lawn mower becomes hypnotic and calls up the emotional memory of the place I grew up: a town of side streets, small, old wooden bungalows with yards, and an abundance of shade trees. Modest, not smug and filled with self-importance like suburbia.

I lean back on my hands and a new line of sight opens up. I see her, three houses down. Even at that distance I can tell she has a nice figure, a comfortable middle-aged body. Her tan T-shirt reveals pleasant curves and her olive drab pants are loose and casual. I wonder about her.

She stands with her arms back, closes her eyes, I think, or at least narrows them, and like a sunflower lifts her face with a mild smile toward the sky's warmth. I am enchanted by her poise, a dancer assuming her stance to begin her performance. What could I really know of her from my place on the steps? The residential neighborhood and two vehicles in the drive, an SUV and a station wagon. No toys in the yard, but kids seem likely. She sneezes.

She moves her left hand forward, and it's one of those moments when life and reality seem contrived; I see the bright spark. For that fraction of a second the reflection is a singular beam of light, a line drawn from her hand to my eye, where it is taken in and recorded but seen by no one else. It must be a very large stone. Could a small one make such a sparkle? But knowing better than to rely on appearances—which always lead one confidently on to err—I doubt a moment and wonder if it had only been a glint off the face of her watch.

Three women come across the yard down from the house and surround her, laughing easily, floating among the curving flower beds of the landscaping with no sense of urgency. For a moment they all look across the yards toward me. I look away, feeling like I have been caught about to do something wrong.

Next to me is a ceramic dwarf, hands locked around the handles of a wheelbarrow bearing a tiny flowering plant. An ant crawls within the orbit of his painted eye. The monotonous hum of the mower expires, and all the smaller sounds re-emerge as if a predator has left the area. Leaves shiver, sibilant and restless above, while birds whistle and sing, and a chipmunk chirps in alarm and scuttles along the cedar-chip mulch at the edge of the house. Moments later the shadow of a cloud dims the colors of it all and another mower starts up farther down the street like a corner preacher who has continued to the next neighborhood to rattle on about the glory of the summer's coming. The cloud passes, and the breeze rolls up its sleeves and blows again, sending maple seeds whirling into the sunlight, moving en masse down the street like an advancing cloud of locusts.

I watch her again. She goes to the street leaving the other three in command of the yard and takes a purse from a car parked there. In a moment she has rewritten herself in my mind. She becomes a visitor. She yawns, mouth uncovered, places a hand on her hip as she takes up her position again a couple paces from the other three.

The story transforms with that single act. Now her patience, her stance at the center of the yard as the others tour the edges and point at shrubs make her not the one who sees that yard every day, but a friend of a friend who couldn't care less. "Nice meeting you," she excuses herself and returns to her car where she fusses a bit with her hair in the rearview mirror before turning the ignition. She drives past me and smiles, and I realize she has been aware of me watching her the whole while.

It is a demure gesture—a safe one, no doubt. I see the empty child seat in the back seat. She mouths "Hi" and continues on, stirring papery whirligigs that rise up and follow her a moment, but then drift back to the impenetrable pavement where they have the misfortune to have fallen.

On a Raft in Green Water

HE STOPPED THE car before a shady gap in the thick brush at the side of the road. The long plume of dust that had trailed behind him caught up and curled around the car slowly before slinking off on a breeze into the woods. A couple of parallel ruts that pushed up a mound of grass between them connected the gravel road to a small red cabin under a patch of sky that showed through the trees above. He got out of the car, his legs stiff from the long drive, and bent with a sigh to remove a large pine branch that had fallen across the narrow drive. He dragged the limb off to the side, its long needles rusty and brittle, and heaved it into the brush where it struck a For Sale sign that rattled like stage thunder.

Up the narrow lane he parked the car in a scattering of acorns among a tangle of tree roots. He felt along the lower edge of the cabin's siding until his hand encountered a key, and then he let himself in. The air inside was stale, dominated by the smell of old furniture. The wood floor was pale, and the varnish had been so completely worn away by passing feet that it was a uniform color except for the very edges and corners of the room. The gleam of the ceiling's wood mocked the tired floor like a photograph of lost youth.

The cabin was a single room with a sink, oven, and fridge along the wall next to the door, a wooden table with four chairs, and a gray couch that jutted out from the wall into the center to divide the space and create a sense of a sitting area beyond it. A television, which hadn't worked in years, reflected a curving room from the corner, and he could see himself standing just outside a sunny patch on the floor, a pale reflection, headless with long legs.

He stood for a moment facing the lake that sparkled at the end of a short, gentle slope outside the bay window. It was his first weekend away from work in quite a long time. Back at the office, people scurried about and complained and laughed and shouted under the pressures of project deadlines and billable hours; the silence of the cabin disturbed him. He opened a window to let in the soft rustle of leaves and the buzz-saw drone of the cicadas. He wound a small wooden mantle clock on the windowsill and dusted it off with his hand; it gave a self-conscious pulse to the room, and he immediately regretted it. The stuffy air, the clock's painstaking etching of the seconds, and the hypnotic hum of the insects outside enclosed him in drowsiness, and wounds opened easily like deep cuts in bath water as he slipped into memory.

Memories were what he had come to find, and yet he stood motionless as though he had discovered an unexpected stranger lying on the couch. Over the past months he had been reflecting on his childhood, mulling it over in his mind as if it were a place he could go for his next vacation. Something of the scent of dust and dried leaves and the way the morning sun slanted through the shivering branches of long-needle pines gave him an anxious flutter of nostalgia.

But the lake had changed. He could see that immediately. The tree that should have blocked some of the glare off the lake was a sheared stump. The lakeside was no longer a verdant tangle of foliage but more reminiscent of the neatly trimmed lawns of the houses of cookie-cutter architecture where he lived. He remembered a song his grandmother used to sing to him. "Little boxes made of ticky-tack... and they all look just the same." Someone had given the small yard a manicure, hoping it would sell the cabin more quickly perhaps. His mother must have hired someone. He shook himself from his trance and went back to the car to get his things.

He decided against the bed in the cramped attic and dropped his bag on the floor next to the couch. No sense setting up camp. He'd only stay until the next day, he figured. He went to the refrigerator humming softly by the door. He hadn't expected it would be plugged in. Inside he found a box of Arm and Hammer baking soda with the top ripped off, several bottles of beer, and a glass bottle of ketchup, nearly empty. He let the door swing shut on its own weight and instead went for a flattened sandwich wrapped in plastic in his duffel bag. He felt as though he were chewing sawdust, so he went back for a beer to wash it down. The silence of the room gnawed at him, and he turned on the old radio on the sill above the sink. Then he pulled down the stairs in a corner of the ceiling and searched the attic for a lawn chair.

Outside in the sun he closed his eyes and leaned back against the plastic straps of the chair that stuck to his sweaty skin. The rising buzz of a cicada mingled with a Billy Joel song—"Honesty" he remembered—and he mumbled along without thinking about it. He loved that song once. He must have been six or seven then. The canned sound of the old transistor radio in the window made the memory even more striking. He let out a long breath through his nose and tried to imagine the music as though it were new unheard material, as though he had crossed years as well as wavelengths to find that station broadcasting from a summer by the lake with the entire family. As though his grandmother were still there with him, still young. Less weight and more color in her cheeks and hair.

He frowned and opened his eyes to dispel the image. Sentimentality stung in a tear that he quickly wiped away, and he felt bewildered and embarrassed, though the only witnesses were chirping sparrows and red-winged blackbirds.

He got up and went to the water and the modest beach that his grandfather had brought there in wheelbarrows years ago in a vain attempt to mask the muddy bottom. His mind drifted back again. In the water, floating in plaid trunks, skin plump and innocent, and those green sunglasses, the green inflatable raft, the green water. A mother younger than he is now. It was a recreated memory, a photograph he recalled. He couldn't have been more than three or four maybe. But the image summoned up emotions that he accepted as memory, the imagined satisfaction of lying in the sun attended by loving hands, guided above the invisible bottom, Egyptian royalty supine across the surface of the Nile.

He had a strong sense of familiarity with that picture and many others. Memories of memories. His mother used to look through them with him when he was a child, turning black pages of photos, some fastened by stick-on corners, others slipping loose into her lap and carefully put back in hopes they would recollect where they had fallen from. Thinking of his mother gave him a warm feeling, distant and disturbingly artificial like one of the photographs of himself that he saw but didn't remember. The song rang like a tin bell now, music a thin stream down a long metal pipe as it crossed two decades like a bad phone connection.

He sat back in the chair, stared through his eyelashes into the glinting ripples, and remembered his grandmother's voice... "When I learned to swim my mother forbid me to go into the water. I had to learn in secret. And actually, when I convinced her I knew how to, I still hadn't figured it out just yet. It was out here. We'd take trips out here to the little sandy spot across the way. That's before Grampa and I bought the cabin. Before we even met. I was just a few years older than you are now. So anyway, I drag her down to the shore and go in really far where she figures it must have been deep but I know the bottom just levels off out there. 'Watch this,' I says to her. And with one foot hopping along the bottom, I make like I'm swimming, you see? Just pushing along with one foot and kicking with the other. And then moving my arms like I saw other people do. At first she seemed suspicious and a little worried, I can tell you. But only for a second or two. And then I stand up, waving my arms like treading water, you see, and waving with one hand real quick like I'm working hard. And she smiles then, and I could tell she was proud... She never bothered me about it after that. And it wasn't too long that I ended up teaching myself to swim just from faking it like that..."

A quarter mile? Maybe a half mile. Not a mile certainly, he thought, gazing from the sliver of dry sand just beyond the feeble waves of the lake on the other side. His father had once swum that lake, straight across. When he was a kid, this impressed him. Standing there years later, he sneered at the distance at first; but as he squinted at it a bit longer, he felt less certain he could actually swim that far. Maybe with someone beside him in a boat, like those English Channel swimmers, but they'd have to be careful with the oars. He thought the crawl would wear him out quickly; maybe the backstroke would get him there. Unless the tiny waves broke across his forehead. If he got water in his nose, it would mess things up. Definitely someone in a rowboat, though.

Another song, faint in the background, but familiar. He walked back up the slope with steps carved into soil and tree roots, back up to the concrete steps at the door. "Wonderful World," an old Sam Cooke song redone by Simon and Garfunkel and James Taylor. Three-part harmony. He thought of it as two-part. Simon and

Garfunkel were their own voice and Taylor stuck out. But not back then. He didn't know any of their names then, just the song. It was funny. "Don't know much about history..." Nor biology, French, geography. They didn't seem to know much of anything, really. The kids at school took mischievous pleasure in a song that seemed so blatantly defiant of the compulsory classroom subjects. Now on the porch he heard it as a sad song of longing. "But I do know that I love you, And I know that if you loved me too, what a wonderful world this would be." But it was unanswered. Does she love him too? Is it in fact a wonderful world? And there was no mention of what kind of world it would be if that feeling went unreturned. What if she chose not to love him?

As he stepped back into the cabin, the radio crackled and whined in a swooping curve of sound, a whistling like the one he associated with war games and radio communications when he and his friends used to run around his hometown neighborhood with dime-store walkie-talkies. "Come in. Do you read me? ...ooohweeeeoooh." He used to imagine it to be the sounds of the radio waves themselves, oscillating into the bent antennae from across the treetops, the hills, with the sound of music riding on their crests.

He and his brother used to carry a Panasonic, blue and round with flat silver circles that controlled the volume and the stations. In fact, it looked more like a small rubber ball. They'd carry it wrapped in one of their grandmother's home-made throw rugs, with a black plastic squirt gun—a German Luger look-alike he realized now—the binoculars with one eye cup missing, and the bird book. His brother might bring cookies wrapped in a dish towel, or crackers, and red Kool-Aid or green in a sealed Tupperware cup. They'd spread the rug out under the inner branches of a pine tree, breaking a few of the brittle ones to make room, invisible through the green needles farther out from the trunk. Home base. Patrols could be run from there. Reports of a blue jay in the Olsons' crab apple tree. Some sour green plunder would need to be collected in case the cookies ran out, which they typically did.

Clothes full of sap, needles stuck to their knees and back pockets, dirty hands and sour stomachs, they'd return home through the gate in the chain-link fence. A Tom Petty song playing from the kitchen window. Mother still such a powerful figure, commanding, sending them in for baths as she wiped perspiration from her forehead with the back of her gloved hand, which still held the spade she had been using to work the soil around the marigolds along the side of the house.

He had spoken to his mother days before coming out to the lake. Her discontent seemed so dissonant. He sought something in her. Her distress, over her father's deterioration and her mother's recent death, was incompatible with sturdy legs, with healthy perspiration which smelled of geraniums and lilac bushes. She lacked that firm sense of control she'd had when he was a boy, the indomitable spirit, "Get inside, you two. We need to be washed up for supper. Let's be ready to eat when your father gets home." He longed to hear an authoritative command, any sort of direction from his mother. But she was older, less certain. Less happy. His memories of how she had been stuck to his mind like the lawn furniture to his skin. The memories were shapes, outlines that he held up before him and tried to impose on what he saw in the present. Images still bright as the young mother in the sun guiding an inflatable raft through glinting crests frozen forever on green water.

He liked beer best when it was as cold as possible. He drank half the bottle before the cap stopped rattling in the bottom of the sink. Out the window through the thick trees and brush at the end of the driveway he could hear the crunch of gravel. The sound gave him a rising anticipation, the promise of companionship. Then a car appeared through the trees, but continued on to one of the other cabins. There were only six on the entire lake, and they were often vacant.

At the door he stopped by the telephone on the wall. He lifted the receiver and listened to the drone of the dial tone for a moment then slipped it back into its cradle and returned to his lawn chair outside. Too late for his mother to get off of work. His father was out on the road. Pharmaceuticals kept him out of the house, and he rarely answered the phone anymore anyway. Something about the physical distance between his parents left him vaguely anxious, and he picked at the label on the beer bottle as he thought of it. Tomorrow the long drive back to Chicago. His anonymous house in the suburbs, isolated by unoriginal abundance. He no longer talked aloud to himself like he used to. His thoughts felt muffled like hearing someone underwater.

"Well, you know how much I hate that cabin."

"Yeah, but... maybe one more year..." he had trailed off.

"I just hate to drive all that way. We never get out there. I don't know how your father can stand it, all that running. I just like to be home. I have so much to take care of here. I take food over to Mrs. Phillips. You remember Ellie?"

"Not really..."

"She needs me. She's not doing too well, you know. Alzheimer's. She keeps forgetting things. I bring her things and she doesn't remember where she put them. And then she gets angry with me. I worry about how much longer she has. And tonight I go for my walk. Every night I walk..."

"I know..."

"They tell me I'm crazy to walk through that park at night, but I'm so sick of that. People keep telling me what to do and I am *sick* of it. I tell you, one of these days, I'm going to just get my own apartment. Just be by myself for a while."

"I just thought maybe we could all get together out at the lake one last time then..."

"I tell you with your father not around, I have a lot to take care of here. Who's going to mow the lawn? I can do it. I'm independent. And people keep telling me I need to be careful with that thing. It's just a lawnmower..."

On the phone he felt the distance, like the radio in the window, reaching him but in a filtered and hollow tone. Mother, I called to hear your voice. She would have her arm around him as they went through the photo album. That closeness, that tenderness, pure love without the complications of working through things, of sex and control struggles, something he hadn't found since. An unquestionable feeling of security without the pouting demeanor of the college girls he had dated or the driven sense of competition and dominance he felt from a couple of co-worker romances over the years. He dreaded the alternating demands for affection and space, the insistence that he understand, and the certainty that he didn't. The relationships always fell victim to the embittered emotional tug-of-war. They always lacked the simplicity of an arm around the shoulders that could shut out the world, or define a smaller one, and keep him safe, content. He feared the open spaces in his life, the emptiness he invariably had to move through on his own. His loneliness was made legitimate when he remembered the comforts of the past, now flattened, two-dimensional like the impenetrable surface of a lake reflecting a bright cloudless sky that is no longer there.

He swatted at a buzzing fly that troubled his head, and then rose to get another beer. He glanced at the bottle opener he had been using. Grain Belt was engraved in its tarnished metal. A forgotten beer. But it sparked something in him. Grain Belt. A bottle cap, on a stony beach along Lake Superior. Cold, in the summer. Skipping stones unsuccessfully into rising white caps. Walking with his brother and his father. Mother is missing, visiting a friend in a small town along the lakeside just down the highway. And there, in the multicolored stones worn smooth by frigid water pounding relentlessly toward shore as though it had forgotten winter was over, lay a bottle cap. Grain Belt. He collected bottle caps. Like he collected everything. Baseball cards, coins, beer cans, feathers from birds at home in the neighborhood.

He used to collect stamps with his father. Very old ones from when postage was only a few cents. They'd send away for them from mail-order companies and then patiently slide them into plastic covers, trimming them with a scissors and pasting them over the appropriate match in a large binder with the words United States Postage Stamps stamped on the front in gold. It seemed impossible to him, the idea of his father being so attentive. The thought of both of them so absorbed in a joint ambition, speaking their own language that even his mother didn't understand, was so unreal now. So many years had passed with stoic hugs and a couple of typewritten letters his freshman year in college. The phone was passed quickly whenever he called, "Hello? Oh, hi. You doing alright? Just a minute; here's your mother. Nice hearing from ya, boy." And if she wasn't home, there was only some awkward small talk. Even back at the university when he had returned to school for a semester with intentions of dropping accounting and pursuing chemistry like his father, the common ground never supported the unspoken bond that once held with only the adhesive of postage stamps.

His father should have been there. Fishing. They should be out in a boat squinting into the rippling water, silently sharing the song of the loon or the mesmerizing buzzings and whistlings of the insects and frogs in the weeds along the shore. He sat with another sweating amber bottle, gauging the distance to the opposite shore. Three-quarters of a mile. Wouldn't he be impressed? Taking after the old man.

He caught his first fish here and many more besides. The bobber dove for the bottom, and the reel whined as his pole nearly leapt from his small but diligent fingers. His father rushed to help. "Here, let me. You got something big." His father took the rod from his hands, stumbling on the rock covered with strands of what he believed was the hair of a mermaid. His father wobbled, and then one foot slipped into the water and the other slipped in on the opposite side when he tried to adjust his balance. Water filled his shoes, but he jerked the rod and pulled in some line with brilliant concentration. The fish breached the surface, but moments later the line went slack. He reeled it in and returned the pole to his son. "Ah... it was a sucker."

"What's a sucker?"

"Bottom feeder. Nothing you want to keep." He slapped him on the back. "Let's get you a new worm there."

He had never really had to bait his own hook. But he couldn't let his father do something like that for him now. He needed to impress the old man, and yet he longed for the attention an empty hook used to merit. The beer grew warmer in his hand, and he finished it with a couple swallows.

"So you keep saying 'MAH-ho, MAH-ho!' We're beside ourselves. Your mom and dad are gone to the wedding and we have no idea what you are so upset about. 'What the Sam Hill's he so worked up about?' I says to Grampa. He says, 'Just let him show you.' So that's what we did. You just keep pointing and walking and you turn around every few steps to see if I'm still there and you say 'MAH-ho, MAH-ho!' So down across the lawn we go and through the ditch. I tell you to be careful because the way they drive through on that road... Well, anyway, I help you across and we go down to Old Cemetery Road and you get all excited - MAH-ho, MAH-ho! You pick up a rock off the gravel road and you look up at me waiting. Then I understand. You wait 'til I pick one up too. And then you turn and point off the road into the ravine. MAH-ho, you say. Mud hole. We took you there the time before you were up to visit, after it rained a whole lot and that area off the side of Old

Cemetery Road was nothing but mud. And you threw stones as far as you could where they would stick in the mud. And you used to get the biggest kick out of that. And you'd wait for me to throw mine and you'd laugh and laugh. And point—MAH-ho!"

He hit his grandmother in the mouth with a cow once. He didn't actually remember doing it, but he felt bad despite the fact she used to tell the story with a hearty laugh. He had wanted his mother, but his mother was at a five-year class reunion and his grandmother was babysitting. He screamed for his mother and his grandmother replied, "Your mother will be back later; go to sleep." And he reached over the railing and hit her in the mouth with a plastic cow he had in his crib.

Squinting into the glinting lake water, he slipped back to her funeral months before, when he had sat thinking of all the things he wanted to tell the mourners. He envisioned himself gathering himself together and stepping into the aisle at the small, crowded country church and spontaneously professing his love and respect for a woman who was a hero and a friend to him. He felt lighter for a moment at the thought and imagined the tearful smiles of the congregation as he apologized for the time he hit her with a plastic cow. But instead he had clung to the hand of his girlfriend who stood tearless and uncomfortable with him in the second pew. He sobbed profusely, and his head pounded with the pressure. They buried her in between cold November showers, and they stood in the red mud under a gray sky that waited sullenly to continue its own lamenting. His head slumped; he only saw the ground, the crisply ironed pant cuffs around him spattered with the red clay of the same soil his grandmother had spent a lifetime working.

His girlfriend. He grimaced at the word. The thirty-five-year-olds he knew didn't have girlfriends, only wives, partners, fiancées maybe. She had left him a month after the funeral. "Morose" she'd called him. He hadn't argued.

He got up for another beer.

He came back down the hill, the cold sweat of the bottle dripping from his hand, and stood staring at the opposite shore. He removed his T-shirt and slid out of his tennis shoes, setting his bottle down precariously on a rock next to the lawn chair. The pine needles stuck sharply in his arch, and he hopped to the narrow strip of sand. He stared at the opposite shore. No looking back, he thought, and took several confident steps into the water. The soft bottom oozed up between his toes and around his feet. A cloud temporarily blocked the sun as he stopped one last time to ponder his trajectory through the cool water. He shivered involuntarily. The water soaked into his shorts, and he hesitated. Only two-thirds of a mile maybe, he thought. The sun returned, and his head felt heavy and warm.

He moved forward until the water climbed halfway up his ribs. Then he dove forward, coming up a few feet farther and kicking out with his feet, slicing the surface with his arms. He made several rapid strokes before he thought to set some sort of pace for himself. A moment later he broke rhythm to lift his head and look ahead, and already he had veered off course. But he readjusted and pressed on, the muscles starting to tighten and feel heavy. Halfway would be soon, he figured.

Among the splashing and his sharp breaths, which came more frequently and awkwardly, he could hear a buzzing sound. Maybe a boat in the water, maybe the beer, or a cicada. He was breathing too hard to effectively keep his face forward into the waves so he rolled lethargically onto his back and pursed his lips as though to keep them just a bit higher above the water. The sun made him squint, and the water covered his ears so that his breath seemed close, loud, swirling through his head with the sound of an aqualung. He alternated kicking styles, trying to save his leg strength. Water trickled into one eye and stung; he squinted it shut for a moment and continued, pushing hard against the cold water that resented his shoulders but then flowed around him and over his heaving chest.

He tried unsuccessfully to keep rhythm once again and then attempted to lean his head back to see where his goal was behind him. He fell back into his faltering stroke, staring at the few clouds in an otherwise empty sky. On a raft in green water. Floating. He glanced down over his nose and chin back toward the cabin. Halfway, he thought, certain of it. The empty cabin stood clearly up the shore. The red siding failed to match his memory of its schoolhouse brightness. Now it looked more the color of dried blood.

The water broke over his nose then up into his nostrils. He snorted and kept at it, breathing hard through his mouth. He felt such an enormous weight, not like floating at all. A jet silently traced a bright white line above the passing clouds. It at first seemed frozen there in its trajectory, but when he focused on it he could see it continued parting the skies, a perfect glowing line that slowly widened like a boat's wake until it resembled a long, faded cloud.

His leg cramped and he jerked violently, grabbing and stretching his protesting muscle and then resuming his faltering stroke when it released again. He swallowed some water that tasted like mud and turtles and something timeless and primordial. He thought about how old the lake was, how it had been there before anyone, harboring life, cold and expressionless, flitting in its shadowy depths. But he remembered warmth. In his head there was warmth, comfort. His body shuddered with each cough, hard and labored. Maybe he was close enough to shore already to put a foot down and stand, but he was unsure and didn't want to know for certain. Better to hope.

He felt something brush his hand, soft and silky like hair, like the mermaid's hair when his father slipped, like his mother's hair how it brushed across his hand as she leaned forward to collect the pictures that had fallen into her lap. Maybe it was his own hair that passed over his forehead. His nose stung; it could have been tears, the sky was so bright. He coughed once more and pulled against the tremendous resistance that kept him from making the other shore. He felt closer than ever. He reached above and behind him like he was pulling himself up. It started to feel possible again and time seemed to slow. He sighed as fingertips brushed his cheek, releasing his fears, easing the struggle until he floated freely again. Everything became effortless. Breathing in cool comfort and feeling the gentle motion, he relaxed, passing over shadowy surfaces on a raft in darkening green water.

Sorting Things Out

HER FACE HAD an anxious look to it. The smile was propped up like many in posed photographs, but it was more than that, something in the eyebrows. They pinched up at the ends in the center as though poised to rise together in distress.

Molly stared at the photo for a while. She felt like she was looking at her own eyebrows, the way they knit together whenever she looked at herself in the mirror and thought her face looked puffy. A look of preoccupation, like a mother seeing her child off to school with a forced smile in the morning but concerned that she looks a bit peaked.

She set the newspaper down and looked across the table at Henry, his bathrobe dipping open to reveal the small hairy patch on his chest. "Did you read this?" she asked.

He looked up from the sports page. "What's that?"

"That murder yesterday."

His eyes returned to the page as he spoke. "I saw something on the news last night. They turned themselves in, right?"

She tensed some, feeling he was shutting down the subject. "Sure, but aren't you curious why they did it?"

"Not especially. Jealousy or something. Maybe robbery. They beat a taxi driver and tied up a liquor store manager."

"That doesn't explain the girl though."

"Well, they were together anyway. People like that turn on each other." She was quiet, and he looked up, a piece of toast in one hand held up for a bite. "Something wrong?"

She stared at him. "Nothing."

Molly set the paper on the table, folded but with the picture of the victim facing up. Photos of the two accused lay curled beneath.

She stepped into the shower knowing Henry would have to leave before she got out. Something about his apathy made her angry. Then she scolded herself. It was just a passing remark; he hadn't been engaged in the conversation. Maybe that was what needled at her. She covered her face with her hands and turned up to the warm water. In her mind she could still see the haunted eyes of the girl. It was as if the photo had been taken with her future murder in mind. The water rushed around her ears, muffling the world for a moment, and she imagined it to be the sound of blood rushing through her head.

She jumped when Henry called her from the bathroom door. "Hon? Gotta go. Quick happy hour with Sal, but back around six."

"Yeah, OK. Don't forget to pick up some hamburger."

"Yeah, I remember."

"Have a nice day," she said after a long pause, but she knew he was already down the hall.

Later in the kitchen she grabbed her keys from the counter by the microwave, and as she passed the table she paused at the paper. She folded it and tucked it under one arm as she stepped out the door. The cold air tingled in her lungs, and she held her breath a moment. Everything was brushed white at the ends with the night's frost; winter's first announcement had fallen to rest on the world.

The morning passed slowly at the office. Molly had to sort through work orders, group them according to clients and projects, and then enter them into the computer. There was no end to it. The stacks came in on a daily basis and waited behind their predecessors sometimes for weeks before they were sorted through. It makes no difference whether I come in or not, she thought. She was standing in a river trying to divert it with her hands. Each sheet chronicled loads of stone, of asphalt, of sand, heavy things reduced to a footnote on a thin sheet of paper. Drivers and their trucks, numbered, weighed, recorded. She should be happy she had work, she thought. So many others didn't have anything. Or they hated their jobs. She didn't hate hers. Not really. What else could she do?

She looked at her purse on the floor inside her cubicle and the paper stuck out endwise. She reached down and laid it out flat alongside her work. Christine. Christine had been studying to be a teacher. What a nice thing, she thought. It was something she couldn't imagine for herself. All those children. Too many to look after. And anyway, she thought, what do I know to teach them?

But Molly knew she wanted children; Henry insisted they wait. The topic came up "like a dog chasing its tail" as he put it. "How can we afford something like that? We still have too much to pay off. I don't want a burden on top of all this."

"Burden? We're talking about a child, Henry. Your child – *our* child isn't some dumb thing you heft around. We're talking about a human being."

"Don't be so melodramatic. You know what I mean. I wouldn't want him growing up without things. Like a decent house."

"There's nothing wrong with this house."

"Are you kidding? We can barely get around each other in the kitchen. Plus, the neighborhood's not much. We should do better. And anyway, it's not a human being. It's a nothing, because there isn't one. It's just your big wish right now."

"And isn't it yours?"

He hestitated. "Not right now. Maybe later."

"Maybe later."

He tried to throw the newspaper he was reading across the kitchen, and it flew open like a parachute and collapsed on the floor in a tangle. "I don't want my kid growing up like poor trash."

"Wait, so now we're trash?"

"No! That's not what I meant and you know it. And we— you know what? Just forget it. We can talk about this later. Now's just... Right now I just don't need this."

She had been pregnant once, years before. She and Henry had been dating six months and had already made plans to move in together since she had been spending most of her time at his apartment anyway. She brought the pregnancy test kit home with her one night, and Henry waited outside the bathroom door that she had left open a crack. She could hear the nervous clearing of his throat moving back and forth in the dark space beyond. When the little blue cross appeared, she opened the door and his face became the surface of the wide empty sea when something turns in the air, that moment of calm that does not comfort, that suggests an unseen storm is moving in or some great invisible leviathan lurks directly below. His eyes followed the cross as she let it fall to the wastebasket and edged past him. They didn't speak again until the next morning, but he held her loosely when they slept. His body felt foreign, awkwardly placed in the bed like a stand-in for another actor.

Henry encouraged her to get an abortion. Weeks later, he asked her to marry him. She often wondered about that child. She must have been about two months pregnant. At the time she felt all right about it. For months even. But later on she started to worry about getting older. Her older sister had died of breast cancer at the age of thirty-seven and now in a couple more years she would be that age. It was a constant worry and she checked herself every morning in the shower, keenly imagining her emotions if she were to find a lump. On several occasions Henry noticed she was upset when she came out of the bathroom. "What is it? What happened?"

"I have cancer," she wanted to tell him. "I don't have much longer." But she'd just shake her head, and he, bewildered, would take her by the arm as she made to move past him. She never resisted and gladly let him close her into his arms, wrap his bathrobe around her for a moment. Later he'd steal glances at her through breakfast. He noticed. He did care. She appreciated that, and the thought made her feel better long before he stopped watching her out of the corner of his eye.

She left her cubicle late for lunch, choosing, as she sometimes did, to eat alone. She crossed the street from her building and went to the diner around the corner. It was a cell phone-free zone. Violators were immediately chastised publicly and the manager rang an angry bell behind the counter. She found it humorous but also appreciated the insulation of those four walls from the rushing cellular world outside where everything was constantly connected to something far away and invisibly bound down.

She ordered a Reuben and ate the first half quickly, surprised at how hungry she was. The day's newspaper lay in disorder at the empty space next to her at the counter. The photo of that young woman stuck out from beneath the folded sports section.

The waitress came over and asked her how her food was. "Good, thanks. Say, did you see that?"

She was in her fifties, blond with a long strand of gray that curved back from her temples and disappeared in a tight bun. Too old to still be waiting tables, Molly thought, and yet gliding back and forth for orders with a youthful sassiness. She leaned forward and looked past the tip of Molly's finger, then slid the sports section away. She tilted her head back a little to peer down through her glasses. "Oh, yeah. Terrible, isn't it? Such a pretty thing, too."

Molly looked again. Was she pretty? The anxious crease to her face was distracting. "I wonder if that's a recent picture."

"It sort of looks like a high school yearbook shot, doesn't it?"

"A bit. But she's older here."

"They say she was studying teaching. Maybe from the night school."

"Could be."

"Pretty thing. Poor girl."

The waitress unfolded the paper and pushed a forefinger over one of the two men pictured opposite the crease, as if she were smearing an insect. The boyfriend, Bruce McWilliams. "That guy looks like trouble. You can tell by looking, can't you? You can always tell a lot by looking." His hair was closely shorn, the way they do to convicts. True, she thought, the picture seemed obvious, as if both he and Christine had their fates lurking in their faces.

Molly just nodded. His accomplice and cousin, Ben Leary, had curly hair, a mild smile that rose slightly higher on one side. Nothing unusual about him but that tiny flaw in the line of his mouth. Can you tell? She wanted to ask the waitress, What can you tell about me?

She wondered how Christine had gotten mixed up with McWilliams. How do any of us get mixed up with the wrong person? she thought. It seems easy enough and common enough that there is no mystery: it's just how things are. But why hadn't she left him?

THE NEXT MORNING the paper lay in wait on the kitchen table like some confidante who had sneaked in the back door, come to speak to her while her husband was in the shower.

The police were releasing more of the details of the murder based on the confessions of the two cousins and some eye witnesses. McWilliams was twelve years older than Christine and had a prior record of robbery. He spent some time in prison for a botched liquor store robbery. He served a couple years in Minnesota and upon his release broke parole and moved south to Arkansas where he met Christine Romero. They dated on and off for over a year. Christine's mother spoke of McWilliams' obsessive need for her daughter. He would show up at three in the morning to apologize for whatever it was he had done, calling outside her window louder and louder until Mrs. Romero would open the door so that the neighbors wouldn't call the police. The situation worsened so that Mrs. Romero finally confronted Christine and begged her to put an end to it. Christine was unsure, afraid of her boyfriend, afraid to leave him. Her mother became angry and told her to leave. She sent her only daughter to live with the man who would eventually kill her.

"What are you reading?"

She jumped in her seat. Henry, in his robe, his hair still wet, looked over her shoulder as he passed behind her. "Jesus, that good, huh? Look at your hands."

She relaxed her fingers where they gripped the page. "It's about Christine Romero."

"Who?" He poured himself a cup of coffee.

"The girl, the murder the other day."

"Oh, right. Did they sort that all out yet?"

She felt a sinking feeling, thinking of how she sorted out work orders all day, thoughtlessly, habitual movement, eventually burying them in a generic folder in a filing cabinet in the back room, forgotten and necessarily no longer important. Perhaps someone in the police department had her job as well, reducing tragedy and atrocity to sheets of paper, folders of reports, measures. "I'm not through reading it yet, OK?"

He smiled at her, "OK, OK, sorry I interrupted." His smile faltered as he watched her lean closer to the page mistaking her frown for a kind of squint. "Are you having trouble seeing that?"

"Please!"

He hunched his shoulders and whispered, "Sorry. Look, when you got a minute, can I ask you something?"

She let out a long sigh and lay the page flat on the table before looking up at him with a sweetened smile that Henry would know to be a warning.

He noticed. "Um... I was talking to Dave about deer hunting this year. We were thinking of taking that whole first weekend in the woods. You know, just stay out there? He's got that trailer. I'd be back probably early Sunday afternoon." Her lips were stretched tight, and he raised the heel of one hand to rub an eye in the moment of silence that he needed to fill. "Now what?"

"When was the last time you and I had a weekend alone together?"

"Aw, babe, come on. We can go somewhere if you want."

"Just not *that* weekend, right?"

"Hunting season is a scheduled event, dear. It's not like I can be flexible about it."

"Well, if it's what *you* want."

"God, is it a crime for me to want things? Can't you get together with Susie that weekend? I don't know, go shopping? Head into Minneapolis for an overnight?"

"And I suppose Thanksgiving you will disappear into the woods as well?"

He hesitated, cocked his head. "No. Thanksgiving is Thanksgiving."

"I'm not sure if my mother is up to all those guests this year. I should help."

Henry brightened. "Well, maybe we can help by not going at all. Fewer people crowding that little house. Why don't we stay home this year?" He went around her and reached down to hug her from behind. "Maybe I want you all to myself." He made a playful growl.

"How can you be so selfish?"

"What?"

"Abandon my mother?"

"What the hell are you talking about?"

"Just go off and run around the woods with your buddies. See if I care."

He stood with his lips pressed into a grim line. "Well, I guess maybe we can just wait to talk about this later." He shook his head and went down the hall to their room. He returned dressed and ready for work, putting his watch on.

"Aren't you going to eat breakfast?"

"No time."

She felt a moment of guilt. That hangdog look, she called it. He put on his jacket and pulled on a winter cap at the front door. Then at the last second as he was stepping out, he looked back toward the kitchen and blew her a kiss. The door closed before he could see her offer an apologetic face.

In the bedroom she looked over at his clothes lying over the chair by the window and remembered how strange and finally frustrating Henry had found her habit of folding her clothes and placing them on a chair or dresser before they made love. His bemused smile the first few times, then the annoyance, and finally the day he'd swept them up and thrown them on the floor with his own discarded clothing. He stood naked and fuming, and though he was ready for an argument, she couldn't keep her face straight. She began to giggle, dissipating Henry's frustrated rage as he stood with his hands on his hips, suddenly aware of his nakedness and posture. He shook his head with a weak smile. "A woman laughing is about the last thing a man wants when he drops his pants."

She sighed at the memory and considered throwing her bathrobe over the chair with his clothes, but instead folded it and placed it in the clothes hamper in the closet. The hamper pressed up against a couple dresses. No matter, she thought, I'd have to have them dry-cleaned if I were ever to wear them anyway. But the closet was small. The room was as well. But room enough for the two of them. There was still a smaller second bedroom, too. Space enough.

She was running late and so on her way out she grabbed the paper. At work in her cubicle she finished reading the latest article before she even turned on her computer. So she *had* left him. She had moved in with a friend. But he had come back for her. He wouldn't let her go. McWilliams and his cousin Leary took her away from Arkansas, kidnapped her it seemed. And yet there had to have been some sort of willingness. The article didn't mention any weapons or struggle, didn't even use the word "kidnapped" or "abducted." She stayed for a time at the cousin's house in Iowa. She could have managed to get out then. Surely the police could have protected her then, and she'd have had a valid response to "We can't do anything until he does something." No, maybe she hadn't entirely been kidnapped. She stayed. In some capacity, she stayed. She was a good person; she was true and devoted. She didn't walk away from things. Or maybe she was afraid. No, Molly thought, she was faithful to a fault.

That night Henry and Molly drove to the hardware store to pick up some paint and brushes. Henry wanted to repaint the kitchen.

"Maybe we should paint the bedrooms, too."

"Why? I don't think they really need it. Do you?"

Molly shrugged. "Remember that secretary Janice, the one from the company picnic? You know, the cute one?"

Henry took his eyes from the road for a moment to see how she was watching him. "The cute one? Well. Not sure. Blond, curly hair?"

"That's the one. I guess she's pregnant now."

"Hm. That's nice."

"Not really. I think she and her boyfriend aren't together. That's the office scuttlebutt, anyway." She stared out the window at the naked trees. It seemed like an eternity since there had been sunshine, though it had only been a couple days. "Sometimes I wonder about this place. What if we just packed up and went somewhere else? Warmer maybe. More sun in winter. I wonder about Florida. All the old people go there, but I figure why wait for that? Enjoy it while we're young. We'd be close to Disney if we had kids. You know?"

She watched him to see if he was listening, and he didn't answer right away. "Where do you go? Where were you just now?"

"Hm?" His eyes opened wide, lifting his eyebrows, and he turned to her with a face that begged forgiveness. "Florida. Yeah, nice winters."

"I wish you'd take me seriously sometimes."

His shoulders slumped a bit. "Honestly, hon, I'm not sure what you want sometimes. If you really want to move to Florida... Do you? Is that what you want, really?"

She shrugged. "Who knows? Doesn't matter."

"Of *course* it matters. You make me feel like I am some kind of monster."

Molly had a cousin in Tallahassee. Not the typical Tampa-Miami-Disney Florida, she thought. But Henry would never leave Minnesota. All his family remained here. Even his grandparents had passed away within a few miles of or even steps from where they'd been born. Most of his friends had gone to the local tech school, and while Henry finished a business degree at the state college an hour down the highway, he came back and took on a managerial role at the flooring business he'd worked at part-time through school. His boss had played basketball with Henry's father in high school.

She fidgeted with the zipper on her coat, watched several raindrops slip backward on the window. She opened the glove compartment. "Have we got any gum?" Inside was a crumpled mass of worn out maps and a silver flashlight.

Molly leaned back and closed her eyes, imagining the events of the last day of Christine's life. McWilliams had parked the car across his cousin's front yard against a tree so she couldn't get out the passenger side and then proceeded to beat her with a flashlight. He split her lip and the blood went everywhere in the car. Then he dragged her into the garage and looked for something to kill her with. The motor oil from the last time he had changed it still lay in a bucket in the corner, and he dragged her there to hold her face in it. She struggled with him, spilling oil everywhere, but he relented. Second thoughts?

Then what happened? How did they get from there to McWilliams' sister's house here in Minnesota without incident? He had just tried to kill her. How is it that the sister hadn't intervened when she saw the blood, the black oozing mess in Christine's hair? Don't women protect women? "I thought it was a Halloween costume," a neighboring witness said. "She got in the car willingly, and I just figured they were going to some kind of party."

Why do men do what they do? What was his motivation? If he hated her, why didn't he just leave? It's not good enough to walk away. They need to erase, to obliterate mistakes, scatter the ashes until nothing confronts them.

Henry was a couple of parking stalls toward the store when he looked back at Molly still sitting in the car. "Are you coming?"

HENRY SAT WATCHING a documentary on elephants in the living room. Molly watched him from the kitchen. He had left the dishwasher open after putting his dishes inside. That bothered her, but after so many fights in the past about such a petty thing, he generally remembered to close it. She already knew without shouting to him that this was, to him, an act of consideration. "I left it open for you. Aren't you about to put yours in, too? Well?" What was the use of fighting about it after all? She got up and rearranged his plate and glass to her liking and placed hers beside them before closing the door. Then she turned to the newspaper spread across the table.

"McWilliams and his cousin then had sex with Romero." She reread the line as if searching for some contextual clue. Had sex? Who writes this stuff? Then Leary shot her in the head at close range with a .22 rifle. The words were clinical and sterile but compelled her to conjure up the tragic drama in her own imagination. Why had they written "had sex?" Could the poor thing have consented to this last act? "*Raped* her, more like," she mumbled to herself. She imagined Christine's willingness of desperation, perhaps thinking she was saving her life. Still battered and bruised, stained with motor oil beneath her nails, deep in her hair, darkened lines in the creases in her forehead. That anxious face now full of terror. She couldn't mask her fear, not if her everyday face like that in the newspaper picture looked so taut with anxiety.

Molly went to the front closet and put her coat on. "I think I'll go for a walk."

"Really? Want me to come with?"

"No," she replied, with a bit of agitation. His eyebrows

rose, but before he could say anything, she added, "I just want a little personal time."

He watched her a moment, then shrugged. "Sure. OK."

They lived in a cul-de-sac, houses circled like wagons on a prairie. She walked to the entrance and then out into the open grid of the city streets laid out in line with the compass. The temperatures were falling below freezing now every night. The last few leaves clung to the cold branches and flapped awkwardly from where they were pinned to the gray wood like faded monarch butterflies left behind by the swarm. The scent of them, scattered on the ground in their first stages of decay, gave her pause. She remembered her childhood, playing in piles of them or kicking through them along the sidewalk on the way home from school. That smell and the damp earth not yet frozen was the last thing Christine would have breathed, Molly knew.

Lying on her back and staring up at the pale sky, past the head of her boyfriend – her *rapist* – and then her killer. Perhaps trying to recall a place in time when those leaves that stuck to the backs of her legs were playthings. Maybe trying not to think at all. Or thinking of her mother back in Arkansas, far away, where the leaves had not yet fallen, back in time where fall was still partly rumor and speculation. Or perhaps knowing she would never see anything beyond this shallow depression in the earth, the surrounding knolls like grave mounds with the black trunks rising up and clawing at the heavens. Invisible to her, just beyond the low ridges was an office park, vacant for the weekend, empty lots, darkened rooms, stainless steel architecture. Pale windows that reflected the colorless landscape. His eyes would have been the same. And his cousin's. No, not the cousin's. Why was Leary there? What part did he have in this?

Leary hated her. His eyes weren't cold but burning with hatred. *She* made Bruce uncertain. It was *she* who made him hesitate. He always stopped to rethink her. And she never cooperated. They had had to practically kidnap her to get her to leave Arkansas. But Bruce couldn't even finish her here, couldn't even pull the trigger, though he had already beaten her and tried to drown her in oil. Bruce sickened him, and here was where he could express that, inside his woman, that weak, sniveling woman. Just a few moments more and everything would be over. "Don't worry, sweetheart," he sneered down at her, but she wouldn't look him in the eye. He bent down and grabbed her by the jaw and shook her face violently, demanding her to look, but by that time the eyes were empty like they had never been before. That look of apprehension, the knitted brow, the trembling corners of her lips were all gone now, and he hesitated.

He leapt up from her and turned to his cousin who sat, shoulders slumped, with his back to them. The gun lay in the leaves, and he grabbed it and laid the barrel under her chin. But now her eyes stared into his. He licked his lips, looked back at his cousin who still hadn't moved. "Bruce. Bruce! Goddammit." He looked back down at her and the corner of her mouth trembled again, but this time it seemed to him it wasn't in fear. It was the beginning of a smile, a smirk. She stared at him, and he could see she was mocking him. He thrust the gun a bit in her throat, and her eyes clenched shut and reopened wide. She coughed, her whole body shuddering with several gasps for air, but her eyes came back to his. He rolled her over onto her stomach with his foot, and two more coughs were muffled by the leaves. He put the gun to the base of her skull and looked away as he pulled the trigger.

Molly's fingers were numb, and she curled them up into the ends of her coat sleeves, taking a moment to figure out where she had walked and to reorient herself for the walk back. She passed a couple of houses with all the lights on, and across the street she could see the pale blue flicker of a television reflecting on a living room wall. The next house was dark like a cave, and when her eyes adjusted, she realized how much light was actually in the sky above. When the night was so terribly cold and dark, the stars became so vivid, the haze froze off.

She arrived again at the end of her cul-de-sac, an illusory street that led nowhere. Almost all the neighbors were home, their lights on, the same flickering behind their curtains. One window still had Halloween decorations up, silhouettes of black cats and witches. She stood at the end of her driveway taking one last deep breath of the dead leaves before going inside, feeling her lungs tighten at the touch of the frigid air. Predictions were for a harsh winter. She dreaded it and wondered again about Florida, what it would be to cross so many states and two seasons, to leave everything dear behind. No one was forcing her to stay.

Moving

CLEARLY THEY WEREN'T enthusiastic. To begin with, the movers were down 40 lira on haggling despite the thirty-kilometer drive out to her place in Eryaman, and to make matters worse, Dilek had made the biggest mess possible with her limited belongings. The two men just stared for a few moments, sizing it all up, the corners of their mouths curled down. Garbage and belongings were indistinguishable, and the two-room apartment reeked of moldy dishes and dirty laundry. I finally understood why she had worn the same clothes for the last three days. Despite having grown stale, they remained the cleanest she had. I, too, stood motionless for a moment, hesitant to step deeper inside for fear of disturbing some sort of archaeological clue. The littered chaos was a kaleidoscope of her world.

It was a world she intended to leave behind with just a couple of hours of stuffing bags and boxes. Sit, she told me when we had first gotten there. We had had an hour and a half before the movers showed up, and she hadn't even begun to pack. I knew she was exhausted. The past week she had shown up at my place each night, long after leaving work. Her hair smelled of cigarettes, her breath of beer. I'd wake from time to time to find her back half-turned to me; I'd lift my head just enough to see her watching the lights of passing cars slip across the opposite wall. She didn't wear makeup, but every day her eyes were held up by dark patches like mascara smeared by tears.

The moving men had shown up a half hour early and with the reduced price they had agreed to, I don't think they had anticipated helping to pack. Both were generic looking men: short, dark-haired, mustachioed, dress slacks not jeans, buttoned shirts, and black leather shoes—what I would categorize as the stereotype of a Turk. The first one never said a word. The other, who seemed in charge, spoke with a voice that kept breaking into adolescent falsetto due to an oncoming cold, and he seemed uncomfortable addressing Dilek rather than the male in the room.

I insisted on helping and stepped cautiously from corner to corner asking what I could do. I collected her CDs and mismatched cases into plastic bags. I tossed whatever was obviously garbage into the corner by the sink. Anything with writing on it went into its own pile, as it was in Turkish and I couldn't determine its importance.

Dilek was confidently in charge. She was a cultural anomaly, and when she had taken me on her search for a new apartment, I stood by, sometimes feeling foolish as she grilled an owner about his place and its condition. The places that weren't worth their lira got her frank opinion before she left. At one building, when the building keeper told her the owner wouldn't take unmarried women as renters, Dilek stared the old, head-scarf wearing woman down and told her she wasn't interested in her thoughts. In a crimson-faced huff, the woman stormed back down the hall and slammed her door. After viewing the place a while longer, we just closed the door behind us and showed ourselves out. It turned out to be the apartment she took after convincing the owner to come to her office to interview her. Her knack for commanding a situation seemed contrary to her role in the circumstances that had brought her to this point.

The movers took a few minutes to size up the load: a bed, some furniture, a stereo. She had a lot of clothes and dishes, plus a small refrigerator rusting in a corner. The movers went downstairs to get a couple of plastic barrels to carry the odds and ends. Through the torn curtain I could see the truck parked two floors below: a small diesel with a canvas tarp over the box. I was curious as to how we would be following them. Either we'd ride in back or take the next bus back into Ankara, I suggested.

She told me this *is* Ankara, a subdivision. But it scarcely resembled the serious capital city with its bureaucratic air and claustrophobic streets of apartments with red-tiled roofs built at arm's length from each other. Eryaman looked more like some former communist country. Tall, unpainted, cement buildings were scattered about the landscape, separated by long stretches of treeless plains like fortunate survivors of bombings in a recent war. Awkward, but functional, and cheaply built. This alone, I thought, was worth leaving behind.

She brought me things to examine, pictures of trips to the Black Sea. "Do... you... want... go? With me?" She held up a beach scene. Her English was getting quicker and was always carefully phrased. I had little difficulty understanding her.

She found more photos and separated them into things to be remembered or forgotten. Ahmet, her ex. Nothing about him looked particularly Turkish. He was a pale, unshaven, lanky man with a long ponytail. Someone you'd expect to find at a liberal arts college, listening to the Grateful Dead and selling weed out of his apartment. An apartment like this one. Now I had a face to go with stories of months of unemployment and borrowing and then stealing money, frequent drinking binges, and a stifling possessiveness. She just shrugged and flung any photos with him in them in all directions across the floor, seemingly unconcerned. But I noticed that she was also digging through discarded cigarette boxes and smoking anything she found.

I helped one of the men maneuver the couch through the door to the elevator. When I returned, Dilek's black eyebrows came together. "I pay one hundred and twenty lira. When we go... for new apartment. You don't help. *Tamam mı*?"

"*Tamam*. OK."

I was watching someone walk through the shards of a former life. I wanted to sort out the pieces to create a picture of my lover who in many ways remained a stranger to me. But these mute things could have been anyone's. A collection of pine cones, from a camping trip maybe, rested atop a pile of books. An empty wine bottle encased in candle wax. Tacked to the stained wallpaper were photos of old friends, better days. Nothing surprising, nothing distinguishing. As I stared down at a collection of worthless kuruş coins in the corner, she embraced me from behind and held something in front of my face. It was the rose blossom I had plucked in passing by the gate of my apartment. Dried and preserved, it would become part of the new layer of artifacts she'd be creating in her new space. I had given it to her almost reflexively when she took me out one night two weeks before.

She was unaccustomed to kindness, she told me. Her father used to spend a lot of time in the smoky *rakı* bars, talking politics, playing backgammon, and lamenting the lack of work. When Dilek was still a child, he'd beat her with the narrow spindle of a broken laundry rack for refusing to wear a head scarf. Her mother had only watched impassively, protected from guilt or mercy by a scarf of her own. Dilek had never given in, and though tears of pain and anger would sometimes escape, she said she never let her father see her break down and weep. It puzzled me how she could have ended up with Ahmet. Ahmet's crimes were compounded by the fact that he had led her to believe, or at least hope, that things were different, that something better was possible.

Leaning against the wall was a plaster sculpture of a man and a woman entwined in a kiss. She asked me how she should move it. I could see a growing fracture along its back, and she was uncertain whether to even touch it. I sensed its importance to her. She must have known its creator. I pointed to a box on the floor, but as she attempted to lift the embracing figures, the fissure widened and pieces of plaster fell to the dusty carpet.

She stared at it splitting in her hands and then let it slip through her fingers. More than its own weight left her then. She nodded slowly, and the vertical lines between her eyebrows faded some. "Not important. We don't take this." She moved with purpose then, and the pile of garbage in the corner grew much faster. Objects, whose only apparent value was sentimental, were discarded.

She kept saying "*At!*" Throw! The flat sound of the "a" from the throat made it sound more like an expression of disgust than a command for disposal. An old picture of Ahmet – "*At!*" To the pile it went. Under the bed I found a pair of leather boots. I slipped them on and they fit me. Ahmet's, she told me. She insisted I throw them away when she saw me in them.

I carried a stack of old textbooks in from the bedroom, rested them by the door, and paused to sip from a warm Coke I had found in the cabinet above the sink. I saw her lean over the chess set at the table. From within a box on the chair, she withdrew a warped set of playing cards and tossed them in a flutter atop the garbage pile. She stared again at the chess board, as if contemplating her next move. She carried the board to the pile and dumped the pieces in a stream, dropping the wooden board finally on top. As she passed, I stopped her and kissed the scar on her forehead where Ahmet had once struck her with his fist clenched about his queen in response to a checkmate.

I hadn't noticed the scar the first time we met. The light was bad, and she held eye contact so long that I felt compelled to look away. I did notice the hole in the side of her nose and the tattoo of Led Zeppelin's Icarus figure near her wrist, partly emerging from her sleeve when she reached across the table for an ashtray. Before living in Turkey, I wouldn't have looked twice or perhaps even noticed. But she was one of the few women I had met there who did not live in the same house with her parents. At that time, these tiny clues seemed blatant social revolution.

My friend Ebru, a singer at a nightclub with a slightly refined clientele, had introduced us and left us alone at a table in a corner suffused with black light that touched off the fluorescent green, orange, and yellow outlines of women's figures painted on the dark walls. We smiled, and I feared we'd just sit and glance at each other uncomfortably. So I stumbled through a few canned Turkish phrases I had practiced: Where do you work? Do you like it? Do you like Ankara? She stopped me early and tossed some back at me, but the loud music, the accent from another region of Turkey, and the very words themselves left me smiling and shrugging. The darkness didn't help. I found I needed the reassurance of sight to understand her.

She smiled patiently and withdrew a pen and a spiral-bound notebook from her bag. She grabbed the unlit candle that rested in the center of the table, slipped her cigarette lighter into the narrow glass for a moment, and we moved together into a small circle of light. Now I focused on her hands and the pen instead of her lips. The pen waved magically over the paper where English words appeared in sharply constructed letters. She had said she couldn't speak it, but she certainly seemed to understand well enough. Her fingers were short, delicate, and her hands were wide. I imagined my palms against hers, how our fingers would line up.

I was reading upside down and she spun the notebook around, nearly knocking the candle off the table. She had already singed her hair in it, and at this she stood and came around, pulling Ebru's conspicuously empty chair up close to me. Through the stuffy air I could now smell something lighter, vaguely floral, laced with sweet almonds, something contrary to a dark bar full of the smoky sighs of drunks and raki's lingering anisette. She curled her long black hair behind her ear close to me, and her eyelashes flicked up as she glanced to see if she still had my attention. She did.

Her name was Dilek, she told me. Turkish for "wish." We exchanged numbers, and within a week we were inseparable.

THE MOVERS GRUNTED another load out the door, taking a chip of wood from the frame with them but not caring. Dilek went around the apartment removing light bulbs. In the bathroom the light had been on the whole while, and she stood on the toilet, trying to balance herself, pulling her sweater sleeve over her hand for protection. One of the moving men, the silent one, returned and beckoned her to step down. He twisted the hot bulb from the socket with his bare hand. The movers went about this job of gathering a person's life into barrels with the same stoicism of the local butcher. With an outsider's eye, I saw a lot of men who walked about unblinking, their expressions dull and dispassionate as they lifted heavy objects on their backs or drove trucks and taxis through traffic that would elicit curses from a patient priest. The moving man pushed past me as I stood in the bathroom door, and he set the bulb down on the countertop. I wondered if they all had such unfeeling hands.

"I... sleep... this." She held up a sleeping mat that had been rolled into the corner as garbage. "She sleep... '*shurda*'... um, at there." She pointed back at the bedroom. Turks have no gender for their third-person pronoun and so in English they commonly mix up "she" and "he." But I then I realized "she" didn't mean Ahmet. "She" referred to the last straw, a humiliation Dilek had endured for too long before closing up this apartment like a crime scene and locking the door for months while staying with various friends. I must have been visibly disturbed by this, because Dilek saw my face and turned to me as though I were the one who needed sympathies and kind words.

"*Bitti.*" Finished. She wiped her hands against each other in the air, the Turkish gesture that often accompanies the word.

I nodded.

When the last barrel had been rolled into the elevator, she stood in the darkened doorway, not reflecting, but struggling to remove the keys from her key ring. She dropped them without pause on the floor inside and walked away. It was I, in fact, who hesitated, not seeing but feeling the scattered mounds of garbage beyond the square of light from the hall and wondering if I should close the door. She waited patiently at the stairs.

Standing by the truck, the two men stared at us over cigarettes as we emerged into fresh air. Without any noticeable sign of protest or discussion of the idea, the silent man donned a jacket and climbed into the back of the truck, and his partner locked the tailgate behind him. Up front in the cab I sat in the middle at Dilek's insistence, and as we drove off, the man bumped me periodically with his elbow as he shifted gears. She squeezed my hand and almost whispered, leaning to the window and pointing the opposite way to Istanbul. She might have considered disappearing into the mighty metropolis with its grandiose histories that made even emperors and sultans into footnotes, but Ankara's low energy still appealed to her. Familiar and comfortable, one didn't need to struggle much to get through a day.

AFTER THE MOVERS left, she brushed off the floor in her new bedroom using a short-handled broom. We laid down the mattress and some blankets, and I poured out some wine from a shop at the bottom of the hill. Unable to find a corkscrew in the piles dumped from the barrels in the living room, we had had the shop owner open it. He used a screwdriver to mangle the cork a bit before finally just forcing it into the bottle. Dilek carried it back up the hill with her thumb over the top.

She washed out a couple of glasses, and we sat with a dish of pistachios, leaning back on each other and the wall behind us. Her room, situated on a rising hill, looked out over the rooftops and was level with the first floor of Kocatepe, the glowing white marble mosque lit up like a castle from a fairy tale. The four minarets stood like Apollo rockets, poised and ready for the heavens. Even a crescent moon, a symbol of the Ottomans, cut through the dissipating clouds up to the left in the window. The perfection of it all made me silent.

"Now all problem finish."

I couldn't decide if it was the translation or her naivete.

"Today you started a new life," I said finally.

"*Evet*. Yes."

The room felt warm, both from the gently gurgling radiator next to the mattress and the magnificent glow of Kocatepe, a vivid and undeniable reminder that I was truly in a different world. She squeezed me and kissed my neck. I sat knowing this probably wouldn't last but not caring.

She said hello as she was already in the habit of doing at these tender moments. "*Merhaba. Nasilsin?* Hello. How are you?"

I smiled, clinking my glass to hers and kissing her rather than sipping. "Very good, now. *Sen? Sen nasilsin?*"

She didn't answer, but merely closed her eyes and smiled. In moments she was asleep.

Small Hope Bay

IT BOTHERED ALICE to know Nora was already up at the house.
After three years Nora had come back with little notice, and Keith had
made Alice pack her things and move them down to one of the
beachside cabanas. It would only be a short while, he said. Alice didn't
say anything, but the sag of her shoulders and her expressionless face
were calculated to let him know she was hurting. She doubted he
noticed, the way he rushed about the grounds looking for things that
needed fixing and sending Abe and Antony around to do the work
while he laughed over rum with a couple of guests.

Alice wondered what Nora would look like. Heavier perhaps,
now that she'd been back in civilization, driving for every little

errand rather than walking. Or maybe the contrary, buff and trim from treadmills and Pilates. Alice stood combing her long hair before the mirror in the cramped bathroom, wondering why guests paid so much for rustic accommodations. The money they spent here could buy them a room at one of the all-inclusive, pampering resorts. Keith loved it, Nora hated it, and the equation added up to indefinite separation. He hadn't explained why she was returning to Small Hope. He probably didn't know, Alice thought.

She took a few sentimental items carefully out of her bag—a framed picture of her and her sister, a small music box her mother had given her for her tenth birthday, and a bone white sand dollar as big as her hand. She had found it with Keith the first time she had ever gone scuba diving, that one week of vacation that turned out to be the first week of her living on the island. She arranged the items on the shelf beneath the window, a bit of decoration as she wasn't sure how long she'd be there. Then she climbed into bed under the rattling ceiling fan, the cheap foam mattress releasing the breath of the sea as her body sank into it.

In the morning she helped Pedro prepare the breakfast buffet, laying out a spread of local fruits that would be exotic for the handful of fishermen. She sliced papaya in the half-light, annoyed that the men had to get up so early on a vacation.

She returned to her cabana to shower, and up the hill she could see a light on at the house. It was the kitchen, and she felt herself release a breath she had been holding. She wondered if Keith had any trouble with his duplicity. He had told Alice it was just for show; he didn't want to hurt Nora.

"What about me?" she'd asked.

Keith sought the answer in his calloused hands. "You don't have to make it like that."

He made it seem as if Alice was being unreasonable. She packed everything into two suitcases, and with the help of Abe and Antony, rounded up the small collection of objects and art that would leave a clue of her presence. They packed it into the lodge truck and unloaded it all into the maintenance shed where it sat among old mattresses, broken deck furniture, and the scattering of sawdust on the cracked concrete floor.

In the afternoon Nora appeared in a sarong and flip flops. Alice looked up from a novel behind the check-in counter and watched her through the slats of the jalousie on the front window. She said the word out loud, jalousie. Jealousy. Designed to shield the people behind them from jealous eyes. Nora scowled and seemed to be angry at the sand for requiring so much more effort to walk across than the handful of slatted boardwalks that connected the main lodge, thatch-covered bar, and dock.

A string of pink shells tinkled against the screen door. "Alice, it's been so long."

Alice wondered how much Keith had told her about what had filled that long absence. "Back for long?"

Alice couldn't decide if Nora's long look was a knowing sneer or simply a thoughtful pause as she decided. "Who knows? Hadn't imagined you'd still be here."

Alice avoided her eyes.

"Still not sick of the island life? Drunk men in love with cold fish and warm rum?"

Alice forced a smile. "Not yet I guess. Beats the hell out of Minnesota. If I never see frost again outside the freezer, that would suit me just fine."

Nora lifted the hinged countertop to pass and found the key to the bar's coolers. She glanced about at the office. "More power to you. But if you ask me, this is wasting away in Margaritaville."

No one drank tequila here, and Alice had conveniently lost the Jimmy Buffet CD at the bar, encouraging travelers to listen instead to music indigenous to the islands: calypso and reggae, scratch bands with roots in the days of slavery and sugar cane, gossipy songs about sex and dirty women. It was Keith's self-proclaimed rejection of white North American transplants that had attracted her. He was accepted well with the locals, and they seemed to respect him—not just as a boss but as a part of the community. During the last tropical storms, he had been right alongside people in town helping reattach roofs and clean up debris, even before he started his own repairs. "I can't have my employees serving tourists at a resort and then going home to sleep in the rain."

Nora, on the other hand, was only tolerated. Though everyone there knew what was going on between Alice and Keith, not one of them would reveal it to Nora. She was the woman who complained at the store when supplies ran out, as they always did, or raged if her groceries weren't bagged properly. Keith was apt to bag them himself rather than have the stock boy called up to the register. When Nora left the island, no one asked Keith even once where she was. They assumed she left for good, or simply didn't care to find out.

Alice had moved into their house the next day with no concern for the ghosts. Now she had been moved out with equal flippancy.

Keith stepped inside the office moments after Nora and merely said Alice's name and nodded in her direction. Alice looked up as though beckoned, but he was already sorting through papers on his desk, paying her no heed. She stared back at the page of her book, the words like lines of ants, orderly but meaningless to her.

Whatever he was looking for, he didn't find. "Well, maybe I *did* leave it in the house. Forget it. I'll look later. Juice?"

"If by juice you mean rum," said Nora.

They walked out, and Alice stared after him for any kind of acknowledgement, a smile, a nod, a turn to stop the screen door from slamming—but it cracked in the frame like a whip, and she felt the sting.

When Alice came to the island, she was 27, thirteen years younger than Keith who nevertheless went about the grounds like a child looking for a way to pass the time, often getting an idea for something new to build for the resort—perhaps even gathering and knocking around some of the materials—before ending up at the bar outlining the plan in an excited voice with a drink in his hand. Alice was on a dive vacation with two women she was working with at the time. She had lost touch with everyone from college and felt she had resigned herself to the effortless friendships of the office, people who had nothing more in common with her than a meaningless job. They had been disappointed when they arrived at Small Hope Bay, expecting organized social activities each day and drunken debauchery by night. But the clientele here sought the simple pleasures of a secluded beach, staring into glittering turquoise and becoming invisible or simmering drunk.

Her friends took a long walk along the beach while Alice sat at the little circular bar in the sand under the shade of rustling thatch. Keith served Alice her drinks, though it was a self-serve bar, and she knew right away he was attracted. When his wife showed up, Alice felt mortified and wondered what impression she had given him or if she had misinterpreted his attentions, like the way he found little opportunities to touch her as they sat next to each other at bar—lifting her wrist to see her watch, admiring her rings by angling her fingers forward as though he might bend to kiss them, or touching her on the knee whenever they laughed together.

She returned to her cabana late that night, and when the darkness among the scattered palms swallowed her up, she turned to see him still standing alone behind the bar, staring after her like the fishermen who stare out over the water without narrowing in on anything, waiting for any movement that might betray the location of their quarry.

Keith, in fact, loved to fish. Whenever time allowed, or a hangover didn't prevent, he arose early and headed up the beach with his gear. Bonefishing was a major draw for half the clients. The bonefish puts up a tremendous fight, and sport fishermen waded into the warm water to stand and challenge them for hours at a time, days on end. The thrill of the hunt was the only prize; bonefish made bad eating and were only kept long enough to acknowledge their capture.

ALICE AWOKE ON the third day in the tangles of a dream. She and Nora had gone casting for bonefish. They stood in the water flicking their lines out repeatedly but finding nothing. They watched each other and threw faster and faster in competition as though the goal were only to move quickly, not to catch anything. The water rose about her, climbed to her armpits. When she looked back, the shore was gone. She stood in the middle of a shallow ocean. The blunt bodies of fish brushed her calves, and her feet sank deeper into the sand. She tilted her head back as the water climbed past her neck until only her nose stuck out. Above her, seagulls hung in the wind motionless, as though caught in time. She awoke with a start to hear the gulls outside her door.

She dressed in a hurry and left the bed unmade. She passed Abe who was carrying a pipe wrench back from one of the cabanas. He smiled at her and nodded. "Miss Alice."

Neither Abe nor Antony would say anything about the present situation, of course, but she imagined them in the equipment shed or Abe with his wife over dinner talking about the most important news on the island. Keith's estranged wife had returned to the island. But what of Alice? That her private life was now likely the center of public attention made her entire body tense with frustration. She pulled a drooping brown frond off a palm tree with a violent tug as she passed.

Alice had always been an unobtrusive type and often disappeared quietly into her surroundings. She preferred things that way, not being noticed. As a child she had spoken very little, and guests at her parents' home were pleased with the little girl who was seen and not heard. She never interrupted them and often disappeared into her room when company came, unlike her older sister who liked to perform, tell the latest silly jokes she had heard at school, or sing a song she had learned on the radio.

Alice's anonymity was robbed from her in high school when over the course of one summer she developed large breasts. Until then she had played the ugly duckling, with braces and freckles. But her uncanny transformation couldn't be missed. Some girls were jealous and expressed their hatred outwardly; others were cleverer and allowed her to hang out with them in order to keep the suddenly distracted boys from straying from the clique. She was always along for the ride, but now she felt like a sort of sideshow. Boys only wanted to cop a feel, and the girls sometimes whispered among themselves and never really warmed to her, never let her inside the small circle. She sat between girlfriends in the backseat like someone who had just been kidnapped.

Keith was the first man who risked it all for her. Alice had had many admirers in college, only interested in her physically, bemused a bit by her long hair that came down to her waist and her passion for literature, but willing to put up with it all—for a short time anyway. Keith was married and so he had something to lose—perhaps more than to gain—in expressing his interest in Alice.

With Nora's return, Alice and Keith's relationship had come full circle. They weren't even a secret anymore; they simply hadn't begun. It was four days since Alice had moved into Number 4. Keith hadn't made any sort of effort to talk to her on even a coworker level, and Alice knew that that silence said too much. At night as she helped Louis clean up the bar and lock up the liquor, she watched the bedroom light up at the house through the bars of the palm trees. When that light was extinguished, hope followed with it.

Affairs have nothing of permanence to them. They drift off like an unmoored boat, collapse under the emotional weight, or explode when exposed to the open air as certain chemicals that must be kept enclosed and shielded. Their romance had started a fast fuse. On an island there is very little private life, and none to speak of at a small beachside resort. But the inevitable drama that would have unfolded was cut short when Nora had suddenly decided to leave. Alice wondered if Nora had been that keenly aware of her husband's shifting allegiance or if they had been observed in some fashion that week. Alice hadn't even convinced herself that something significant was going on. But when Nora had left, the path became clear.

BY THE END of one week, Alice was certain she was being tested somehow or being sent a message. He must have said something, perhaps a midnight confession when spirits and sex loosen a man's tongue. Nora looked her right in the eye each morning as she walked into the office.

"I slept just divine last night. Wasn't that breeze something? I forgot how much I liked that part of the islands. The nights, you know? All that heat in the day, and then the way the sea just... I don't know."

"Breathes?"

Nora looked at her with distaste. "Sure."

By noon Nora would be drinking rum beneath the rustling thatch and staring out at the sparkling water over a book she never seemed to read, a romance novel from the book swap in the sitting room at the lodge. She decided to go topless and lay in the sun drawing surreptitious glances from the three middle-aged men who were there for bonefish. Alice, with much more to offer in that regard, scowled at her, and for a fleeting moment she was inclined to take off her top as well in childish competition. Keith approached Nora from the dock. Alice caught her breath and felt something drawing away from her, like the sea along the shore slipping back into another wave. He stood looking out to sea as though trying to see what Nora was seeing. They spoke, but Alice couldn't hear them, and she watched Keith's lips move in profile as Nora's sun hat tilted up and toward him. Suddenly, he bent down and his face disappeared beneath the brim. Alice imagined the kiss, a peck of resignation.

Nora had always played the mother to the reckless child, calling Keith home when he had too much to drink and threatened to stay up the whole night with a group of rowdy anglers. But Alice liberated him from that, gave him all the lead he wanted, let him run. Sometimes she played right along with him, downing shots of Barbados rum and dancing to Bob Marley while the men wanted something more familiar to their tastes. If she turned in early, she was asleep before he climbed into bed.

Nora used to appear with arms cut in sharp angles over her hips, a hiss off her tongue as she sent him from the bar into the office to shut it down for the night. When Alice asked

Keith for a job at the front desk, he readily agreed, perhaps thinking that would be one less task for Nora to send him off to do. Alice returned to Minneapolis with her travelmates and within a week was back on the island with two large suitcases to start a sudden life in the Caribbean. Food and shelter were already taken care of. Security would soon follow.

Daniel Bundy, Keith's grandfather, had been a merchant marine, and in his travels throughout the Caribbean, he had come across Small Hope Bay. The crescent of shoreline was so named by a famous pirate who believed there was small hope of anyone finding his treasure there. Back in his sailing days, Daniel and some fellow crewmen had found the place empty, a perfect place to build a fire and spend the night under the stars and a warm blanket of rum. After he retired, he returned with his family; one of his old shipmates had bought a plot of jungle and built a couple rental cabins. Daniel returned there every winter from Miami, and the business passed through another generation's hands before a hurricane leveled the property. Keith saw it as an opportunity, bought the land, and built eight cabanas using pine he had to ship in from the States.

Alice found it strange to be enclosed by pine in the Caribbean. In her backyard where she grew up, pines rich and dark scratched at the wind. The only trees that didn't withdraw from the cruel winter, they stood like sentries at the property line in a neighborhood of orderly streets—curbs and gutters, roads with edges, roads that did not disappear under a sudden deluge. Houses were laid out with elbow room and manicured yards, which seemed like Victorian gardens compared to the chaotic tangle and spread of sea grape and mangroves. The beaches showed a long line of filth like the edge of a dirty bathtub. Each day she watched Abe and Antony rake the detritus from the sand to make it look like a postcard again for the guests.

Her sister told her how lucky Alice was that she had escaped from Minnesota and was living in paradise. But Alice had doubts that slipped around beneath the surface the way a fish is hidden behind the reflection of the pure blue sky, just the smallest of ripples betraying its presence. Paradise shouldn't seem so constrictive, taunting one with clear boundaries and yet a distant abandoned horizon. Islands are false sanctuary, succor from stormy seas, safety after a long journey. But in time one finds oneself trapped like Crusoe or Caliban or confined in illusory comfort by Calypso. The undulating edges of the water become as unyielding as prison bars. For the first time in three years, she looked at the situation with a pessimistic eye—she was being held in the blue fist of the sea.

Alice sat at lunch with the three fishermen at one of the three long tables. Behind her were Keith and Nora. Alice spoke softly—and at times incoherently—as she strained to listen in on their conversation.

"So you're from the Northwoods then? Long way from home," said one of the guests, a portly man named Richard who insisted she call him Skipper. From the way his breath labored at the slightest effort, she feared his red face might mean more than too much sun. Skipper wore a fishing hat full of lures more appropriate for the region to which he was referring and sported a cheap Hawaiian shirt. What did Hawaii have to do with the

Caribbean? she thought. A cultural invader. As if all the tropics were generic and homogeneous, anonymous screensavers with white sand and a palm tree. Margaritaville indeed.

"If home means below zero, I prefer to be as far away as possible."

The men laughed, a little louder than anything humorous she said demanded. She saw it often. She wondered if they were always like that in the presence of strangers or if this was just something she brought out in people. These men were all middle management or mundane salesmen with maybe twenty years gone at the office or dealership, off to pretend to be sportsmen for a week. She tried to imagine the wives left behind and whether the men would be happily received when they returned.

The clucking of Nora's tongue drew Alice's attention. "And the little hussy tells me she graduated from such and such university as if I should be impressed, and all I can think is 'Did they teach you to dress like a slut around the office?' These interns are simply dreadful."

Alice flinched at the word "hussy" and mumbled in repetition, "simply dreadful." Who the hell speaks like that? The balding man with the awful sideburns sitting across from her – Doug or Don, she forgot which – looked up at her. "Pardon?"

"Huh? Oh. So you're heading out with a guide today?"

"Yep. Up to the north shore I guess."

"Nice. Don't forget your sunscreen."

He grinned foolishly, rubbing his hand across his shining skull, and Skipper slapped his back with a hearty laugh. Grinning apes, she thought.

Keith spoke around a mouthful of food. "I never could stand a place like that. All those stuffed jackals and 'esquire' after their names. Some kind of inferiority complex for lawyers. Can't call them 'Doctor,' but god forbid they be associated with the rest of us title-less common folk."

Nora replied, "Just relax. I left them there. We're safe in your little fortress from reality."

Alice chewed her food as slowly as her mind did Nora's words, carefully sorting through them for the meaning beneath. "Left them?" "We?"

Nora had been pampered all her life, an East Coast princess who schooled in the Midwest where the Coasties often sent their snot-nosed prep school kids in hopes they might discover a little down-to-earth humility. Alice believed it rarely worked and had known Nora's type in college. They joined the most prominent sororities and dressed the same, talked the same, spent the same.

Nora met Keith at the University of Wisconsin and started dating him almost as an act of rebellion. He was a business major, not terribly interested in being there, and really just finishing out a degree while working part-time as a carpenter's apprentice. Keith had told Alice, with mocking disdain, of the handful of times he had taken Nora out for a couple beers with his co-workers, the "townies." Nora had been shocked by their lack of refinement, these people who wiped suds from their upper lips with the back of a sleeve or openly ogled and flirted with any woman who walked in the door.

They married sometime after that, when Nora was in law school. Law school itself was superfluous. Nora had an ample trust fund and would never need to apply for a job. She could work for the family firm and make incredible amounts of money for a mediocre performance. None of it really impressed Keith much, and he had told these stories to Alice as they lay naked at night under mosquito netting. Alice didn't mind him talking about her; she wanted reassurance that what had happened had really happened, and for good reasons. Over the course of the first year, the stories dwindled away until she was left with the illusion that the house, the resort, the island, Keith— everything was her discovery and always had been.

Nora's father never liked Keith but kept out of his daughter's business, at least as far as Keith had seen. Money was always available, and there were hard times with the floundering resort when Keith had needed Nora to back him up. Knowing that her father disapproved was enough reason for Nora to persist. Keith explained to Alice that this is a ridiculous game of the wealthy. Children who never know risks or limits pretend to live a life on the edge just to spite parents who really only care about the well-being of the family's image. Failure in this arena had nothing to do with money. There was always plenty of that to go around -- and a parent, uncle, cousin, or grandparent who had more than enough resources to bail someone out. "Melodrama," said Keith. "Always certain that their 'struggles' were center stage in the world. Nora could raise hell if anyone asked her to swap her spa appointment, like it was the sky falling, and completely lose it when the locals couldn't make it in because they still hadn't cleaned up their shattered houses after Tropical Storm Whoever wiped them off the map." He feigned pulling his hair out and Alice smiled, laid her cheek on his sweaty chest, and curled her fingers in the hairs there.

Alice pined for those late-night moments when he'd confided in her, but then when she really thought about them, she couldn't remember how long it had been since they had really talked. What was going through Keith's mind now that Nora paraded around the grounds once again? Did their legs entwine at night? Did he run the tip of his finger lightly down between her breasts and give her gooseflesh?

Each day that passed, Alice tried to convince herself of Keith's innocence in all of this. His intentions somehow must have been good, and soon something would give. Nora would return to the States, and Alice would easily move back into the life they had been living as if nothing had happened. But doubts slipped in through cracks in her resolve.

She had created illusions much as the travelers often did, the ones who came to the Caribbean really expecting paradise. What a shock then when nature washed up that long line of rotting palm fronds, dead fish, and plastic bags on the gleaming white sand. How could it be that there were voracious mosquitoes and sand flies and no-see-ums in the Promised Land? And the relentless heat stifling one's breath, the heavy humidity, thick and sticky on the skin, the sudden torrents of rain that covered the island as if it were being pounded into the sea. "Why wasn't I told it would be like this?" they'd cry in the main office. Some even demanded a refund or a discount.

Keith wandered past and smiled at her briefly, like greeting an acquaintance in the street on the way to the post office. Alice stopped a moment, half-turned to address him, and then, feeling exposed in her need, hurried on, discreetly glancing into the shadowed screen windows of the dining hall to see if someone had witnessed her humiliation.

She wanted to ask Keith if he understood what she was feeling. She wanted to know when Nora was leaving. *Was* Nora leaving? It all looked too convenient and comfortable. Alice had just been holding her place, keeping the bed warm, running the office while Nora stepped out for three years. Then she began to suspect that Keith had known more than he let on. Just one phone call all of a sudden and Nora would be there in a few days? Impossible. Nora was impulsive, of course; wealth allowed for not making plans. But it didn't seem likely.

Alice hissed at Keith as he walked past the kitchen door and beckoned him over. "We need to talk." She felt a tremor in her voice but wanted very much to hide it.

"Now's not the time."

"And when is?"

"Things'll work themselves out."

She squinted at him. "You have no idea how long she'll be here, do you?"

He looked put upon, and wagged his head. "The place is part hers anyway. What can I do?"

"Small Hope is kind of a funny name, isn't it?"

"What?"

"There's small hope of me ever getting the hell out of here."

"You're being melodramatic."

"Where would I go?"

"Home? Hell, how should I know? You have hotel experience. There are hotels everywhere in the world."

167

"If I didn't know any better, I'd say you wanted me to go."

"You are the one talking about getting the hell out."

She flushed, simmering with anger at herself for always losing the battle of words. She knew she was smarter than Keith, but he was agile with his tongue, quick in a firefight. Once she had taken his line of argument, she was lost and ended up manipulated into a contradiction as glaring as the beach at high noon.

"We can't talk like this. I have to go," he said.

Alice stormed out the back door of the kitchen.

THE NEXT DAY Alice sat with her novel under the thatch roof of the gazebo at the end of the dock. Nora, her sarong rippling in the breeze, walked out toward her with a plate of fruit in her hand.

"Nice little spot you have here."

Alice hated the tone of her voice, how Nora could make all the people around her seem like children she was barely tolerating. She sat on the railing and stared at Alice. Alice ignored her, and Nora quickly dropped her roundabout approach.

"I know."

Alice paused, but stared at the page.

"Did you know that? I knew the whole while."

She looked up from her book with a weakly guarded innocent look.

"About you and Keith. Before I left." She skewered a fleshy red piece of papaya with her fork and used it to point at her. "I allowed it. You were my ticket out of here." She watched Alice carefully, but Alice did everything she could to prevent even the tiniest muscle movement in her face. "He didn't tell you? I'm sure he didn't blame you. He was happy to see me go."

Alice cleared her throat, and Nora stopped a moment, waiting for her to speak, but nothing came.

"Quite funny when you think about it. We both used you in a way." She punctuated the statement by popping another piece of papaya into her mouth like the cherry off a sundae. Alice just stared at her, unsure of what to say but careful to keep the rising rage from betraying her. Perhaps this was a bluff and Nora was testing a suspicion. Nora filled the silence, "Sure is quiet around here, isn't it?"

Alice started to nod slowly, and Nora took it as assent, when in fact it was resolve. Alice closed her novel, stood up, and looked back down the dock to the shore. But instead of walking away without a word, she turned, and with all her might flung the thick paperback squarely into Nora's nose. The plate flew up into the air, out over the water behind her, sailing like a discus, and for a second they both seemed to be watching it to see where it would land. But Nora's half turn toward the arcing disc was more to see where she was about to fall. Her arms reached toward Alice but were already out of the shade of the gazebo and over the water. Her legs kicked up and one of her flip flops flew and hit Alice in the chest. She caught it and was suddenly alone, clutching the flip flop. In the water below, Nora was thrashing about and screaming for help. It wasn't very deep there and a nearby ladder led back up to the gazebo, so Alice just peeked over the railing and dropped the flip flop, watching it twirl down to land flat on the surface a few feet from Nora. Nora's face was a swirl of blood and seawater, and she wailed, "You bitch, you broke my nose! Bitch!"

Alice said nothing but walked back down the dock. Antony and Abe came out of one of the cabanas to see what all the commotion was. The three fishermen were at the bar, drinks half raised as they watched the spectacle. Lionel, the local cab driver, had just dropped off two new arrivals and stopped on his way to his car. Keith came out of the office, and when he saw Nora flailing in the water, he ran to pull her out, brushing past Alice with only a pained glance and a muttered "Jesus Christ."

Alice signaled to Lionel who opened his car door and sat inside out of the sun to wait. Abe looked at her wide-eyed. Antony allowed himself the briefest snort of amazement and started walking toward the dock to assist.

ALICE STOOD WITH her suitcases at the end of the town dock, watching the men unloading supplies as if stockpiling for a war or a hurricane: crates upon crates of produce, beer and soda, canned goods. A shipment of car tires rested on a pallet at the stern. They were almost done but would have to wait until the island's mail showed up. Then she could climb aboard and settle in somewhere for the seven-hour crawl to the next island.

"Going somewhere?"

Alice didn't respond to the question. Marco, the island's only full-time police officer, stood over her, rubbing his chin distractedly with his hand. He stared out at the seagulls holding themselves up on stiffened wings, surveying the goods for something loose and edible. "I got a call about an incident out at the lodge."

"Is that right?"

"Yeah. We looking for someone right now."

"Any idea who?" Alice thought Marco was skirting along the edge of good humor, but he didn't smile, and she looked down at her hands folded in her skirt.

"Some." Marco lifted a wave to someone on shore who shouted his name. "The whole island know Nora is back. She cracking the whip already. Law and order, you know."

"Marco, please, you can't—"

He held up his hand to silence her and then brought both hands to his hips. "I was rather surprised to see the mail get out a little early for a change today."

Alice looked out at the boat then up at him, but she couldn't see his eyes through his sunglasses. "Thank you," she whispered.

Marco gave her shoulder a squeeze and walked back off the dock.

The side of the boat was streaked with white beneath the spots where the seagulls typically perched. The rest of the hull, the railings, the gear, the little crane--everything showed patches of rust, and the whole vessel looked like a sharp object, dangerous to the touch. This was the product of paradise, the sum of time soaking in the sea, being battered down and baked by the sun. It all took its toll on things, and she looked at her tan hands and the skin stretched across delicate bones that reminded her of her mother's. There wasn't much else she was taking. Like a child covering her eyes to make the world invisible, she readjusted herself on her suitcase and turned toward the end of the dock so that only the sea took up her field of vision. The next island was out there somewhere, neatly folded into blue, but all she could see was the empty horizon.

Picking Blueberries

I WATCHED HIM roll out of bed directly across the hall from me in his sagging white T-shirt and underwear. His pale legs, which hadn't seen sun in more than half a century, took the floor firmly, and he pushed himself up with one arm. Then he shuffled and muttered past the doorway where I couldn't see him getting dressed, not that he gave a damn if I saw him or not. I got up as well, knowing that otherwise I would receive periodic knocks on the door frame and comments such as, "Anytime you want breakfast, you let me know," which were really inquiries as to when I was going to "get started," as if the day were a task to be taken on.

It had been nearly a decade since Grandpa had taken over the top spot on a list that had never been written down, but which most people knew: of all the most aged residents in the county, he was the oldest. When anyone came by the house for a cup of coffee, with perhaps a dash of Canadian Club for good measure, he used to show them an old black and white hunting photo – a dozen men lined up hefting rifles in the air with an equal number of lifeless deer sprawled out in a row before them. None of them smiled over their prizes, as if members of his generation were somberly aware that their colorless images would long outlast their mortal days. "I was over at Joe Patka's and they gave me this, 'Hey, Jack, you ever see this picture?' And I look at it, 'Of course I remember that.' And then he says to me, 'You know you're the only one in that photo's still alive?'" He doesn't mention it anymore; it goes without saying. It sits in a short stack of photographs curled like yellowed leaves above the cold fireplace next to the mantel clock.

Grandpa came into the kitchen, planted his hands on the sink's edge and looked out of the windows to the north where the morning sun was already reinvigorating the red of the barn. After a long moment, he hitched his suspenders up over his shoulders, nodding, "Yah, looks like a good day for it." Berry picking, he meant. He often groaned and struggled up out of his armchair, but several hours hunched over blueberry patches that didn't even come up to his knee never seemed to bother him. I imagined that many of his aches and pains were ploys for sympathy or attention, and it troubled me as much as it annoyed.

His old friend and fellow berry picker Bob was up from Chicago, a place like Rome to many here, a sort of seat of the empire of the Midwest: all roads led to it. Years ago, especially during the toughest times up here in the Northwoods, people disappeared for work and seldom returned, an immigration of a much smaller proportion than the one that had brought my grandparents halfway around the globe. Chicago natives, in turn, often venture north, seeking the quaintness of the small town: cars left running parked outside the butcher shop or the bakery; clerks who would just as soon have a lengthy chat about recent trends in summer weather as ring you up; gas stations that are full service where a teenager, wearing an old Shell baseball hat with black fingerprints along the creased visor washes down the car windows, while inside the kids press their lips up to the glass and make faces. The big city tourists are faithful to their big city life, but something of the green places is always lacking, and so they trade the shadows of towering concrete for the dappled shade of maples and oaks for a spell. They gulp the precious air as if they've come up out of a stifling cave, and their faces go blank as the breeze through the leaves and the swaying hay fields erase the hum of humanity. But few of them ever convert. They pass through here like they're on safari and return after a week or a weekend to tell their friends about it.

The sight of an Illinois license plate often elicited a rolling of the eyes. So it was almost culturally dissonant when someone like Bob, who spoke the local language and still kept a house on a road named after the family, showed up from the Land of Lincoln.

I, too, am a deserter, off not in search of work or greener pastures necessarily, but on a mission to see how far away I can get. But every summer I come back feeling like an empty pocket, contrite and deflated, looking to pass a few days, a few weeks, maybe a month. It is a peculiar place for me, always something fresh and renewed, like springtime, yet laden with childhood memories, pensive and reflective like a dark winter night. I come to seek the pastoral solace of sweet grass and songbirds as much as to open a vein and wallow in the gut-felt mourning of time's loss. I have a much keener eye for the horizon behind me than for the one ahead, and I work at melancholy like a tongue pushing on a sore tooth. I am a soul divided, I suppose.

My grandmother, now ten years gone, sent me into the larger world and yet calls me back every so often. Her fascination with the exotic pages of *National Geographic* and books about faraway places infected me when I was very young, though she had never actually gone any farther than the big city for work, and even that was years ago, before she married and settled into the farm forever. My wanderings became a sort of tribute to her, a duty to fulfill her own dreams. I walked through the pages of those magazines, touched the stones and idols of the civilizations that had only come as close to her as the county bookmobile. Since her death, I have felt lost beyond those glossy photographs, rootless and drifting, seeking a month or six of work at a time, always in a different town, a different country. And sooner or later, I come home to see Grandpa.

Bob showed up an hour after breakfast, a cane in one hand, a small pail in the other. He had a round, thick face like a pumpkin, and the silver stubble on his cheeks had about a day's start. A John Deere baseball cap sat on the back of his white hair as if the wind were about to take it, and his brown eyes had a milky shade to them. Smiling, he came up the cobblestone walk, checking his footing with a downward glance every few steps. I didn't really recognize him. We saw each other so infrequently that we mutually existed only in Grandpa's stories. "I wouldn't've hardly known you. When was the last time I saw you? Jack tells me you just come back from—what's it?—Guam?"

"Guatemala. Yah, the berries ain't so good down there." I liked to slip into the local tongue: grammar of convenience and matter-of-fact.

After a round of weak coffee, we piled into the front seat of Grandpa's truck. He pulled out slowly onto the worn asphalt without a glance to either side, and I leaned forward to look into the passenger mirror to see if anyone was flying over the hill behind us and taking us by surprise. It was a county highway, but there was no rushing Grandpa. It occurred to me that maybe he shouldn't be driving at all.

Just down the road a stretch, we turned onto crushed gravel and entered a confusing labyrinth of access roads through "The Barrens." Back in the logging days, the lands in all directions were clear-cut, and the profits whisked away by a few lumber barons. They, in turn, drew arbitrary acreage lines and sold off what appeared to be a desolate battlefield, sight unseen, to immigrants looking to climb into daylight out of the iron ore and copper mines an hour or two east of here. Some of it was OK for farming. Some acreage was marred by ravines. All of it was full of stumps. The immigrants, mostly miners by trade, were happy to have land of their own and the sun on their backs, and they rolled up their sleeves to dig in the earth again. They broke the red clay and coaxed out crops until a couple of generations later, the stubborn clay, in turn, broke them. A few family farms still struggled on. But no one ever tackled The Barrens. Among rolling fields already considered poor farmland, The Barrens had been considered hopeless and left for dead. But Nature scoffs at ideas of what's fertile and what's not. Now a thick forest of birch, maple, and scrub brush opens into small meadows here and there, laden with wild-flowers in summer. And the sandy soil along the roadsides offers sweet wild blueberries for anyone who knows where to look.

Grandpa could spot blueberry patches from the driver's seat without turning to look, while I squinted at the roadside foliage with darting eyes and shook my head: "I don't see anything." After a couple of days, I would learn to read this language of the land a bit, and the subtle shades of green and motley patches of sunlight would speak to me as well.

I sat between the two old-timers. Bob would kid my grandfather and then nudge me as we waited for his reaction. Grandpa sailed through a stop sign without even slowing. "Hey, Jack, you know that was a stop sign? You don't want the Pilsen police up here to give you a ticket."

Pilsen, unincorporated, has no police; in fact, merely a hint of a town, it consists of a tavern and a half, and half a church on a bend in the road in the middle of nowhere. I felt Bob's bony elbow push at my ribs. Grandpa didn't blink, smile, or hesitate. "I don't need to stop; I put that sign there." And he had. He was part of a crew, along with a few from the hunting photo, who put their backs into cutting these roads during their stint in the Civilian Conservation Corps camps back in '38. He'll tell you about it if you ask. Sometimes even when you don't.

Both of my companions had stories, and if you heard them enough you could see the patterns, like carefully crafted and rehearsed routines. Tales of manual labor that put the fear of the capitalist in you, even before they told you how many cents they were paid a day. Back-breaking work: laying railway ties and digging ditches or hauling rock. Much of it sounded more like punishment than work in these modern times of machines specialized to the task and union-protected construction workers who could take the winter off if they were smart with their pay. And then Bob had the war stories. He had been a gunner on a B-17 in World War II Europe, and with little invitation he chuckles and shakes his head through a few tales, as though he too were incredulous: shrapnel lodged in his helmet; unfortunate compatriots slumped, lifeless in a copilot seat; crash landings, one of which left him in his ball turret on the runway sans plane; the Brits shouting, "Yanks go home."

He looked straight ahead at the road but spoke to me and Grandpa with little sideways leanings of his head like a stalling metronome. "Jack found my cane out here, isn't that right?"

Grandpa nodded, and a faint smile emerged on his lips. "I don't know how a guy who needs a cane to walk can get so goddamn far before he sees he forgot it."

Bob shrugged, "We looked for that gall-darn thing for a couple hours. Now I always keep it in arm's length."

"We found it the next summer laying right where he left her, I guess."

Despite his bad knees, Bob would get down on all fours in the underbrush to hunt the low-lying blueberry. You wouldn't know they're there, they're so unobtrusive. Just some brush in a ditch and then a tilt of the head opens up a line of sight, and you notice them all of a sudden. The earth opens up and holds forth an azure feast, a clever poker player revealing a flush with a grin.

The wild blueberry is a touchy type but so much better tasting than any of the domestic varieties, which are fatter, bluer, and full of watery flesh. I've twice tried to take some plants home with me, carefully digging up the earth around them and transplanting them to a spot I estimated offered about the same amount of sunshine and drainage as the place I had uprooted them from. Not a chance. For some things, where the roots lie is more important than anything.

The truck rolled to a stop halfway into the middle of the road, and Grandpa just parked it there. I suppose it didn't matter. We set into the ditch and began foraging for berries, and it made me think how primitive it was, hunting and gathering. Just two generations back these folks were poaching – not for fun or defying the law, but for food shared among neighbors. My grandmother had known what mushrooms wouldn't make you retch and could make a coffee substitute with the dried roots of weedy chicory along the road.

After a while I paused to straighten my back, marveling at how this eighty-nine-year-old man could remain bent down in work for such a long time. Years of practice. What's picking blueberries compared to chopping and hauling cords of wood, plowing fields, hoisting railroad ties, stabbing at the hardened clay with a shovel? There was a strength in him still, despite the long armchair diatribes against a body that didn't serve him as it used to. He took off the straw hat that kept the sun off his bald patch and wiped his brow with an old red handkerchief before blowing the dust out of his nose into it. His remaining hair was closely shorn, tiny silver bristles riding sharp over the hard contours of his head, the liver-spotted scalp a tight patch in the center.

My pail was already filled, and I went over to check his. He looked back and forth between them. "You got a smaller pail." He looked at me for my reaction, and then his lips curled up revealing teeth as worn and worked as the rusted and crumbling machinery that stood scattered in the overgrown fields behind his barn. "Hey, Bob. Look how much he got." Work completed was a badge of honor. I often thought how the callus-free cubicle and computer work must have appeared frivolous labors to his generation. But he never faulted me for it. "I'm sure glad yous kids don't need to work like I did," he'd say, never in a self-aggrandizing tone, but with real gratitude.

When we decided to move on down the dirt road, Bob was the last one to the truck, and my grandfather muttered, slightly annoyed, "Probably saw another goddamn berry across the ravine." Bob was a die-hard.

We stopped in a few more patches and rounded up about five quarts of berries before calling it a day. I returned to the truck complaining as much about my back and knees as the two octogenarians. We passed through Pilsen on the way back to the farm. Bars and churches. The twin temples of small town Northern Wisconsin. Buddy's is the first building at the town line -- a true tavern, complete with a variety of furry heads on the wall and Grain Belt beer light. It had been a local favorite, and though one of three town structures, it wasn't originally built there. The flood of '38 or '40-something washed it off its foundation out near Badfish Creek, and they hauled it with horses to the place just across the county highway from the farm. There are no posted hours, and I can't remember the last time I saw a car parked in the gravel out front.

The other bar—or half a bar—is a real roadside attraction. There's no name on it, but the locals call it the Plywood Palace. It's a wonder of physics and architecture, how it stands up to the cutting winter winds. As its nickname implies, it's cheaply built. There's no running water; the barkeep brings a 10-gallon bucketful of dishwater each day to wash the glasses. The gaping holes in various places make it seem as though a couple of drunks had nailed the whole thing together with scraps from a woodshop. Even the concrete slab it wobbled over was incomplete, with open packed dirt patches in a couple of corners. Parking was in the flattened grass of the field out back, where there was also a lot of room to pee. One bottle of blackberry brandy stood behind the bar, and the fridge was stocked with cans likely purchased from the grocery store in town.

Grandpa looked at it as we passed and shook his head. "One time a guy goes in there and says, 'Hey, bartender give me a six-pack of beer.' 'Can't,' he says. 'Well, why the hell not?' 'I'd be out of beer!'" Grandpa gave a wheezy laugh, but I believe it. An oil heater keeps the place open through winter for snowmobilers and a few farmers feeling cabin madness rising up like the snow outside their windows.

Even the church doesn't feel whole. Every other Saturday afternoon, the priest from the next town over gives mass. Headstones in the "New Cemetery" out back outnumber parishioners. A few stones bear names of family, my grand-mother in particular, and my grandfather with the finishing date left off. Grandpa, in fact, dug the first grave there, all by himself with a shovel, for Joe Kovalik, one of my clan. He got paid less than what rests beneath the cushions of the couch or "davenport," as we call it. Prior to that, the dearly departed were laid out in the "Old Cemetery," a quiet clear-cut square in the woods about a mile from the church. Only folks from Grandpa's generation can read the epitaphs there. Older grave markers made of wood have rotted away, and there are wide stretches where no one puts in new graves for fear of driving a backhoe into someone's forgotten forebear.

The land up here is a swirl of ethnic flavors, like inner-city barrios spread out over acres. The Finn Settlement to the north; Croatians on the farms around the crossroads to the south. We're mostly Slovaks and Czechs, in and around Pilsen – eaters of cabbage rolls, bread dumplings, sauerkraut, and kolaches. All the roads are called Janiczek, Pagac, Sedlak, and various other Eastern European surnames, a registry of original residents across the plat maps. Grandpa speaks with a "th" that sounds suspiciously like a "d." There's a tattered copy of a Slovak ABC book in a box in the basement. Like many his age, he didn't speak any English until he went to school at the age of six, and he dropped out to help on the farm by the eighth grade.

The name Pilsen crossed the ocean with the trunks and uprooted lives that set out from the Old Continent over a century ago. Plzn, of pilsner beer fame, still exists in what many in our community still call Czechoslovakia, never mind that a country by that name no longer exists and hadn't yet come into being when everyone emigrated back in the late 19th century.

Bob took up the narrative as we turned into the yard. Among the names in these stories, the non-Slovaks always stand out, so few in number that they could be named by their ethnicity without confusion. "Remember the old Polack? Had that place up over on Lajcak Road? He owned the little county market out past the Trestle." With a capital T, this meant the largest of the bridges, where the train used to pass over the deepest of the the ravines before the whistle-stop in Pilsen. "Good man, that guy." He paused a moment, perhaps as curious as I was about what had sparked the non sequitur.

Bob and Grandpa carried the berries inside where they dumped them on a sheet laid over the bed in the third bedroom and spread them out "to let 'em ripen some." Grandpa had his system. We walked Bob to his car and watched as he worked his cane behind the seat and then lowered himself in awkwardly. "We going again tomorrow?"

"If it don't snow."

Bob chuckled, repeated that to himself, and took a wide turn over the edge of the lawn to get out of the driveway which was bigger and wider than many convenience store parking lots.

Grandpa headed over to the corner of the garage where the downspout from the roof disappeared into a blue 50-gallon plastic barrel full of rainwater. It looked more like a stagnant pond, full of floating insects and concentric mossy stains up the sides marking the varying water lines. Every evening he'd fill a ten-gallon pail from the barrel, carry it to the garden, and with his right hand, use an old Folgers coffee can with nail holes pierced across the bottom to scoop and drizzle last week's rain across his garlic plants.

Despite his years, he never had that air of waiting to die, but rather waiting for something that never comes, like many of his companions from years ago, no doubt, lined up waiting for work. In fact, it seemed even now he waited for the same. Work defined him, and without it he sank into moments of nonbeing. It was painful to watch. In the summer he could at least poke around the garden and water the garlic. His garlic was a masterpiece of cultivation and a bit of a local spectacle. The bulbs came out the size of baseballs. He hated the stuff, couldn't stand the smell, much less the taste, and gave it all away at harvest time. It was proof enough for me that he simply enjoyed the work. And the attention he got for it didn't bother him any either.

He stood watching the water disappear into the cracked clay as a pickup truck drove past. The driver gave a wave, and Grandpa just lifted his chin once in reply: Joe and Mary Janiczek, from the hilltop farm a half a mile down the road, the nearest neighbors. Their son Mike and his wife Sally were just another turn past that along the county highway; another son was out past The Barrens with a small dairy farm, not far from his sister Lucy. The grandchildren had moved into nearby towns, the kind with post offices, maybe a half hour away. Only one of them, the youngest daughter Agnes, moved away back in the '70s, far away to Chicago for work. She was dead within a year, struck by a reckless boater while swimming in Lake Michigan. Up North, boating accidents are nearly weekly events in the summer, but this tragedy left the family unwavering in their distrust of wandering too far from the homestead. Some families are like oak trees, spreading roots deep and dropping the seeds at arm's length.

Ours, however, appeared to be more akin to the dandelions in the yard that Grandpa didn't "give a shit about," taking to the wind and landing where they will, touching the earth lightly. That bothered him, as he was the one true exception, still wearing out his shoes on the walkway between house and barn that his father had laid out with stones turned up by the plow. Children, grandchildren, and even great-grandchildren now had come and gone, stayed some years, some days, and left him alone to contemplate a silence he had never known in this place.

That night Grandpa brought up a case of Mountain Dew from the basement and carefully cut it open with a kitchen knife that had been sharpened so many times its blade was narrow and undulating. But it always cut like a razor. I would have simply cracked the glue on the flap and ripped it open in a single motion, but he patiently manipulated the worn blade like a surgeon to remove the side of the case cleanly. He reached into the cupboard and brought out an oversized plastic bottle of Canadian Club whisky and poured a finger of it into a glass. He kept his back to me and grew quiet as though I were witnessing a secret. Years ago he drank too much, his angry years I called them. Much of that anger had left him when he stopped. His hand trembled as he lifted the heavy bottle up to its place in the back of the cupboard. He muttered "Goddammit" at his unsteady grip and shuffled into the dining room with the glass and the soda can without meeting my eye. Then he settled into his armchair and turned the news on, louder than bombs.

I sat down at the table and ate some of the berries distractedly, whole handfuls, barely savoring them as I rustled through a newsless newspaper. I heard him chuckling, and I looked up embarrassed, imagining what I looked like as I ate. "You better slow down; you're turning blue."

He leaned back in his recliner and uttered the long, existential "yah" that accompanies the sighs in these parts, possibly a hangover of "Ja" from the Germans. He stared up at the ceiling before turning back to me, causing the vinyl to creak a bit. "You know? I'm getting old."

I sensed him slipping melancholy a bit; the alcohol loosened his grip. I winked at him, "Nah, not yet."

But he ignored my levity. "It's awful lonesome up here. Summer's not too bad, but the winter... yah... Wasn't so bad when Ma was alive..."

All of the family missed my grandmother; she was our keystone. Grandpa would occasionally mutter himself to tears surrounded by the quiet farm, the product of so many years of labor and sacrifice, and lament the fact that she had never had time to enjoy it. Part of that was his fault, his temper, the anger reaped of the hard life and a hard family. It just wore her down over time. My thoughts turned dark whenever I thought of what my grandmother must have endured with him. But then I'd think of how he had suffered with his own upbringing: his sickly mother; an alcoholic and brutal father who had died young; siblings who sounded more like competitors for survival than blood relatives. He wasn't the first born, but rather the oldest of those who lived to their teenage years. He took on the role of running the farm, leaving it for city work for a spell only when it was necessary to support the family. As years passed and everyone abandoned him, he got married and started his own family. Things didn't get much easier and his temper, born of frustration and sore muscles, grew. He never took kindly to braggarts and, though he wasn't a brawler, I'd heard about at least a couple of times when he'd balled a fist at an insult and set things right in the tavern down the road.

I never really sorted out a judgment for him. My feelings were mixed. In the end, I guess I just chose to suspend it altogether. He was Grandpa after all.

"I sure do enjoy coming up here. The air is so good. And, of course, the blueberries." This grabbed a subtle smile from him.

"Jesus, you sure can eat the berries. You know, if you ever wanna move up here, that'd be OK. You could take your uncle's old room. I wouldn't charge you rent or nothing." He quivered with a silent laugh.

"Yeah. But what would I do up here? There's no work."

"Yeah, that's right," he replied, grimly, without a pause, already knowing the obvious.

It always came down to work. Most of the waking hours of his long life—and probably many of the restless dreaming ones—had been consumed by labor, either the actual grinding of bone and muscle or the worry that the next day the work would run out. There was a short time when Grandpa, too, had to venture from home to find something. He spent a couple of months in Chicago, deep in the earth like the miners in the family before him. Not to dig ore, but to make space for a subway he'd never see or use. "They had to put pressure down there so it wouldn't collapse. Eighteen pounds. Guys'd come up with their ears bleeding." His remained intact, but his time in the Windy City was short. "Then my dad got sick. He had an enlarged heart, you see. They needed me to come home and take care of things. No one else would do it. They said, 'Let Jack go.' He died not too long after that, and then I had to take care of the whole farm myself. There was just me and your grandma. And my ma." And then she, too, left. She sold him the farm and went off and remarried with a widower, someone who had been similarly fated to lose a spouse in mid-life, a childhood friend she knew from the old village. Lendak, Grandpa called it, but I've never found it on a map.

He looked up at the clock on the mantel with a start. "Why don't you see if the game's on? I think they play tonight."

The knobs on the radio had come off but it didn't matter; there was only one station that broadcast the game, and the radio was stuck on it. He would simply plug the thing in at 7:00 on game nights and listen to the color commentary of his team's frequent defeats, all the while lamenting the lack of equity in the league before finally dozing off to greener ballparks. They were the Braves before the Brewers, just another old friend that had moved away. The radio crackled to life, and I imagined what it must have been like without television, when the mind was called to bring up images to the words, to do all the work itself.

The next morning I woke up and wandered into the kitchen, lightheaded with wisps of the previous night's dreams, all of them obscured, only the emotions of them remaining, a sense of longing. I filled a glass at the sink and stared out at the barn, now much smaller since Grandpa had downsized it after the farming years. It was a small wonder to me; I could barely drive a nail straight into a two-by-four and he, without any sort of blueprints or sketches, could dismantle a full-sized barn, trim it this way and that, and put it back up, the roof turned ninety degrees from the original and one story lower. Same old wood, same concrete slab, same windows even. Just some new shingles and a fresh coat of red paint and white for the trim, and there it was, a miniature barn that looked too proud and smug between the rotting chicken coop and the sagging-roofed garage of the same but faded colors. Beyond them were the fallen combat craft the color of burnt blood, jutting up from the tall grass where they had been left behind when he finally gave up his battle with the land. They were relics of harder times, labor memorials. After the armistice, it didn't take long for the surrounding forest to reclaim most of the hundred acres, everything except this little corner.

I squinted at the willow tree between the garage and barn. It was a mammoth sprawling trunk grasping the earth, stubborn, old, but split up the middle like radius and ulna. It had been born on the farm before my family even set foot on the continent, somehow spared by ax and saw. Grandpa, concerned about the split trunk despite all the years it had been like that, often grumbled it was time to bring it down. Other trees around the yard hadn't lasted a month before he had followed through on his threats, but this one always remained untouched. Grandpa and his siblings must have sat in its shade and swung from its branches, so I wondered if this stay of execution was a rare expression of nostalgia.

He almost never brought up his brothers and sisters, and the silence about them fed my curiosity until I asked once. "Danny fought in the War," he told me, "got the Purple Heart. One of *them*," he referred to his estranged siblings as such, "took it, I guess. I can't imagine what the hell they'd want with it. What does it mean to them anyway? It ain't theirs." He waved his hand in disgust, ending the matter. "Yah, Danny, he just didn't wanna work on the farm." A world war seemed like quite a rotten way to go about getting out of some heavy work, but what did I know of those times? I read somewhere that the Romans enjoyed war in that it was a sort of recreation, a break from the real horror of tedious and pointless labor, which rarely offers up a victor or a hero like battle does. "He says to me, 'Jack, I'm tired'a this place.' So he leaves me here with Ma and everything. They all did." Danny came back from the war a somber, limping man, with smooth bubbled flesh where the floating fire had touched him when his boat went down in the South Pacific. He got married and left again. He died not long after of a heart condition like his father before him.

After his father's death and before Danny's, Grandpa got married and my grandmother moved out to the farm. I've seen pictures of the little house, the color of tar paper, grim like the faces posed beside it, slightly out of focus in gray and white. Faces were rarely sharp. Even the smallest motion of the subject took the edges out of them. Sometimes an arm or a face smooth like smoke, they looked like ghosts passing through the vivid farm set. And now they all are, in fact, just that, except Grandpa. For him, those structures of peeling paint and tattered tar paper, the simple tractor and plow still rustless and poised, are the haunting spirits.

"Morning," he said like an announcement more than a greeting as he came to the double sink and grabbed the empty coffeepot from the dry side.

"Good day for it?" I asked.

He nodded at the window, and I wondered if he ever saw the yard the way I did, like a memorial. "Yep. Looks like."

I patted him on the back and felt the solid muscle there. His paunch sagged over his belt, and he had filled out to some larger pants in the past few years, but the hands still hung like heavy, blunt tools. His shoulders still seemed capable of bearing burdens. No doubt about it, he was a hard man, and, in his day, no one to get cross with. He still kept a rifle under the bed, mostly for the occasional bear, he maintained, but if a robbery appeared in the news he was quick to point out the gun's presence and promise that he'd take care of the sonofabitch OK who ever came around looking for trouble. It made the rest of the family nervous, that gun lying around. My mother feared the day he might mistake someone in the family for an intruder. We never stopped by unannounced.

He sat down to wait for the coffee, his slippers propped up on a footstool, his hands folded in his lap. I tried to imagine his days of spit and vinegar when he'd take on a full day's work like it was his imagined trespasser. In the old photographs he was never smiling, whether he was standing with his little kids in front of the new house he had just built or hoisting some lake trout worthy of film. Even his wedding pictures had a dark, grim air to them. Something in his angling eyebrows made his face look sharp and edgy. He was grumpy from time to time and had a few pet topics—in particular the local priest's frequent financial sermons and the brand new camper trailer parked out behind the church—that sent him on blistering diatribes. But other than that he was a teaser and often channeled a moment's anger into sarcastic remarks.

An occasional tight-lipped silence from my mother or one of her brothers was enough of a hint at how things used to be. My mother barely let slip a word of those days of full-on thunder and lightning. Just insinuations like, "You kids don't know what my mother went through," and "you don't know what it was like." I always protested that it was her silence that kept it so. But it was her right. She was torn between her desire to preserve – or at least create – the idyllic grandfather for her kids and an honest need to accuse him as the cause of all the bitterness of her childhood and of her mother's life. As I sat by the window trying to imagine where they had slid the original tarpaper shack of a house into the ravine when this one had been completed, I knew that it wasn't us at all that she was protecting. Most of modern psychology seems hell bent on rending the painful memories from a person's sealed vaults and putting them out on the table to look at, as though by trying to forget, someone was shirking a responsibility. In my mother's case, perhaps a deep wound needed to be sewn shut and left to harden over with the scar. I, on the other hand, can think of nothing that better inspires a story than rolling up a sleeve or pulling up a shirt and tracing the crooked flesh left from the day you made it out alive.

A loud bashing startled us as we sat across the table from each other, both lost in our thoughts, and I nearly spilled my coffee. It was Bob banging on the aluminum screen door with his cane, and we got up like field workers called back from break, leaving the half-finished mugs to head out to The Barrens.

"Isn't this where the Kovac boys had their accident?" We were rolling up a short incline to cross the now defunct railroad corridor. Ten years back, they tore up all the railroad ties that both these men had had a hand and a back in laying out. Now it was a snowmobile trail in the winter and an ATV playground in the summer.

Grandpa kept his eyes on the road straight ahead, "Those damn three-wheelers, they come running through here like hell. Don't slow down for nothing."

I asked, "Was it serious?"

His disgust rumbled in his throat, and he frowned as if it were a passing tick, "Ach! You couldn't kill them boys with a gun."

Grandpa pulled up in front of a small clearing sparsely populated with a handful of pine saplings; I could see a few blueberries resting in the half-shade of a couple of them. He grunted his consent, pulled his pail from behind the seat as he got out, and we all got down to work. I watched him for a while, his thick fingers stained from the day before and turning darker still. Much like bruises, the color lingered for a day or two, reminders of the experience. We would talk about the day's berry picking in the comfort of the living room long after the muscles stopped aching and our bellies were full.

After a half hour of picking, I was thrilled at the amount of berries I was getting, but Grandpa shook his head. "There's just no berries like years ago. That goddamn DNR keeps spraying up here. There used to be a huge patch out there along the Corridor; we'd fill an ice cream pail in ten minutes. Nah. We'll go up the road some."

We climbed back in the truck and continued on. The tires kicked up gravel, which clicked and pinged against the undercarriage, and a long plume of dull red dust rose up over the road behind us before slinking off into the underbrush. "Jack, I think we just passed some there."

Grandpa ignored Bob and slipped a cassette into the player and turned it up a bit. It was the only tape he had, some kind of polka collection, a group that had passed through several years back for the local summer festival. Every July everyone from the surrounding farms gets together for a softball tournament and a drunken cookout. Sometimes a bit of polka as well. A half mile down the road, after a couple of weak protests from Bob, Grandpa finally stopped the truck. "Let's see if we can find some here."

I hadn't really noticed or given it much thought when I was a child, but I grew up on ethnic food – pierogies and dishes that I've never seen on a menu in a restaurant. Somewhere within my average American upbringing, I still carry the threads of another culture. The farm had become a country, the country of Pilsen. Not Slovakia (or Czechoslovakia). Not the USA. A wave of yearning souls had founded it, and now, like all empires large or small, it was taking on a slightly different shape in the hands of the next generations. All that remained for me, perhaps, was a handful of recipes and a broken accordion in the corner. And Grandpa.

Grandpa stood for a moment, pursing his lips. "Things aren't like they were. No," he said to no one in particular. Then he straightened his straw hat and bent over the ground before him again to resume his silent hunt.

The silence was expressive. Enough said. There are berries to be picked.

Thirst

PATRÍCIA STARED OUT at the horizon where the highway turned liquid and evaporated into the sky between two distant hills. As she plodded across the empty fields, the sun beat down on her dark skin and her limbs grew heavy. She stopped to rest. Juan, absorbed in watching the flopping motion of his untied shoelace, nearly walked into her from behind.

Pay attention.

He nodded. She held out her hand, her eyes still fixed on the horizon, and Juan handed her an old dented canister wrapped in threadbare canvas the color of dried mud. She tipped her head back to swallow the last mouthful of water so warm that it passed through her lips without seeming to touch them. She handed the canteen back to her silent companion who squinted up at her, unsure of whether she offered a swig or simply expected him to resume his duty of carrying it.

The canteen was Juan's most valued possession. It had been given to him by strangers some months before on a day that felt like Christmas. No, more than that. Christmas had never been like that day. Not for Juan. The children had gathered in uncertain anticipation outside the compound. The truck had rolled in, trailing a cloud of dust, and fair-skinned strangers had emerged speaking a mysterious language. English, he was told. From the United States, in the north. He remembered hearing of these people from the television. Rich, violent, they lived where everyone owned a car and carried a gun for protecting it.

The rusted hinges on the trailer door had made a hawk's screech as the door swung wide, and the light had glinted off the bounty waiting there—toys of every imaginable kind. A soccer ball still in the box, board games, dolls, books, a paddle game, a bat, a stuffed animal with one eye missing, a radio, even a bicycle with two tiny wheels dangling off the hub of the back tire. More things than Juan could count.

Juan discovered the canteen among the tumbling treasures, and from that moment, his solemn stare never strayed from its target. He recognized it from old movies where people fought in terrible wars and crouched in dusty trenches and drank desperately from these things. He waited in anxiety as the first groups formed lines, taking turns at claiming their gifts. He held his breath, fervently praying to the Holy Mother that this one object be spared for him alone. They started with the youngest first, girls before boys. Juan took his turn with the six-year-old boys, which meant he had to wait through two groups of five and under and then the six-year-old girls. But the canteen evaded the onslaught of desperate and grateful fingers. He wiggled his toes inside his shoes. He couldn't believe his prayers had been answered.

He jumped forward when his teacher nodded. Victorious, he clutched the canteen in both hands, hanging back under the eaves, outside again where the others kicked balls, squirted each other with neon-colored guns filled with water, and where a group of girls threaded bracelets with tiny bits of plastic from some kind of kits. His probing fingers felt the rough fabric and then tested its worth by pressing harder along its surface, feeling every seam, every dent in the metal below.

One of the strangers approached and spoke to him in Juan's own language but the way only some of the very young children spoke. Es por agua. The man pointed and slowly reached for the canteen, all the while watching Juan's eyes carefully. Juan hesitated but relinquished it to smooth hands.

Look. Um, *mira*, he commanded. Juan looked up at him first, then back at the canteen. Along the top of the canister the man grasped the lid, twisting it off to expose the dark hollow inside, which the man made a point of showing to Juan. Ah - gwa, he said, louder this time. Perhaps he is hard of hearing, Juan thought. Or thinks I am.

Agua?

Sí, sí. Agua. He showed his large white teeth in perfect

rows, none with darkened blemishes, and summoned over one of his companions, a woman in bright red shorts and a white T-shirt with the sleeves rolled up and some words written across her chest. They spoke wildly in their strange tongue and then just stood looking at him and smiling. The man held out the canteen for Juan, but with a hesitancy that suggested to Juan that there might be a condition for its return.

Can - teen.

Juan hesitated, then grabbed his gift and took one step back.

Gracias. He bowed slightly. The strangers looked at each other and laughed.

Day - nah - dah.

Juan endured a slap on the back that stung a bit but then ran inside to put his new discovery to the test of water. From that day forward, the canteen played an important part in their daily patrols...

Patrícia sighed, and without looking at Juan, began to walk back toward the compound. Almost as a parting thought, she called over her shoulder for Juan to follow. There would be no bandits today. It was almost time to eat. Juan followed over earth cracked and faded like the tired skin of an old man.

AFTER BREAKFAST and morning prayers, Patrícia and Juan set out to continue their patrol for bandits and rebels. At the edge of the field, out behind the compound, Patrícia lifted the wire and its rows of crooked teeth for Juan to crawl under. Goats stood staring at them in the sparse fields. Across nameless land and several barbed barriers they ventured into unscouted territory. The ground sloped a bit, and they came to where rains of long ago had cut a meandering scar through rock and soil. The arroyo was deep but empty, a dried vein thirsty for the blood of the land to run through it again from the quiet mountains in the distance. They climbed down steep banks into a river of sand and scattered stones.

Juan searched through the worn rocks for ones that fit his palm snugly. Good weapons, he figured. He nodded sagely at several as he hefted their weight before concealing them in his pockets. Patrícia warned him that too many might slow him down should they need to make a quick retreat for reinforcements. The distorted silhouette of a hawk flowed silently over the cluttered path in front of Patrícia as they followed the jagged arroyo, pausing to listen at each bend. As the sun rose, the shadows that protected one side of the gully slipped slowly into the sheer wall that towered over them. Juan followed patiently and squinted up at his sister with a certain admiration. He waited, clutching the canteen.

No one was sure whether Patrícia really was his sister or not. No one except Juan. He just knew. They had arrived at the orphanage before Juan could remember. Patrícia, who was believed to be only five at the time, simply appeared out of a cold night; a quiet ghost, she stepped into the circle of light at the back door, struggling to carry Juan under his armpits, face forward, like an offering. He wore only a soiled diaper that sagged with its weight. Juan's wailing brought the staff out into the parking lot where Patrícia stood grimly in the cold wind that blew down from dusky skies to beat her tattered dress. No one knew anything of their origin. Patrícia, though capable of speaking, did not. They were treated as siblings and Juan never questioned it. Only Patrícia may have really known the truth, if it mattered.

Agua. She held out her hand. Juan scampered up, unscrewed the top and watched Patrícia's soft throat pulse as she drank deeply from the canteen. Juan took one swig for himself, tightened the cap, and returned the strap to his shoulder.

Patrícia held up her hand. In the distance she heard the sound of loose gravel scattering beneath the roar of an approaching vehicle. The sound grew closer and closer before finally grinding to a halt somewhere just above the rim of the arroyo. Dust passed overhead, momentarily dimming the sky. Hearing voices, they both froze, only their eyes searching the sparse clumps of dried grass along the edge above their heads. A car door. Then another. Footsteps in gravel and dirt. Words indiscernible and then the faint smell of cigarette smoke. Juan pulled at Patrícia's arm and pointed directly above them. Patrícia scowled and shook her head but pushed herself flat, back against the dirt wall. Juan followed her example.

They blended, motionless, like chameleons, until even the swallows took no notice of the two silent figures and flitted in and out of the holes carved into the baked mud above their heads.

They could hear laughing. Closer. Another car door opening and then a slam. Footsteps. Steady and purposeful. A soft noise, barely audible in the breeze. A panting rhythm somewhere between a whimper and a whisper. Juan looked up, squinting in the bright blue sky. Dust tumbled over the lip of the arroyo and fell into Juan's face. He bit his lip and wiped at his eyes with grubby fingers.

Suddenly, the air split open with a loud shot and they both jumped back against the earth as if struck by a blow. A sound like all the sounds in the world being summoned together in one tiny instant and let go with a burst. The blast could be heard retreating back into the world across the land, the hills, and even fading off into the mountains. The swallows fled like bullets from their nests. Patrícia clutched Juan's arm until her knuckles turned white; her nails dug in like talons. Juan wet himself.

Juan's ears rang but he could still hear the yelp that had almost blended with the gunshot. He covered his ears, trembling, the sound at once surprising and out of place, and yet shapeless and familiar memory. Another shot and Patrícia's nails dug deeper into his forearm as she pulled one of his hands down from his ears. Tears traced gleaming tan paths down his dusty cheeks and fell to the dry earth between his feet. He wanted to cry out but fear made his throat as empty and parched as the arroyo itself. His impulse was to run but his feet were firm, his knees uncertain. He gave no thought to the weapons in his pockets.

He looked to Patrícia, and she appeared blurred and frightened, her eyes squinted shut. Then footsteps through the ringing. Several. Coming closer. Patrícia and Juan cowered against the dirt.

Then someone counting, uno - dos - tres. The sun blinked for an instant. All the terror of midnight passed in that frightful second, and from the sky the dead fell. The stones of the arroyo clattered like dry bones and when Juan dared to look, a couple of meters to his right, the glassy eyes of a dog stared back at him, the head twisted in an awkward and uncomfortable angle. From Juan's lips escaped a staccato cry, brief but audible. They sensed a pause above them. Then the ringing of metal being locked into place and the dog made an epileptic leap to the sound of thunder. Neither child could hear now; their ears had become numb and muted as though submerged in the earth behind them. They both cried as quietly as possible, praying for the nightmare to end.

They stood there shivering in the hot sun for a long time. Shadow seeped toward them, a sheet of oil slipping over the stones, reaching halfway to their side of the arroyo before either of them could move or even speak. Juan's pants were almost dry and began to smell.

Patrícia cautiously looked about for a place to climb up the wall of the arroyo so she could search for the enemy. Juan could only stare at the gaping mouth of the dog, at the torn flesh that no longer oozed crimson, at the mangy patches that spoiled the rest of its lifeless hide, and at the solitary black fly that already drank from the glassy pool of a vacant eye. He shuddered until Patrícia returned, jerking Juan's arm to break his horrified stare.

They are gone. She complained bitterly of not having binoculars as a proper patrol should have so that she could have searched the horizon for the identity of these bandits that would so mercilessly attack such an obviously pitiable animal.

She started back home, turning to Juan who was no longer trembling but had lowered himself delicately to one knee several paces from the limp figure.

Ven, she commanded with just enough conviction that Juan obeyed and followed along.

HE RAN. The sky loomed behind him, a threatening, purple cloud billowing down into the arroyo. The walls on either side grew higher, stretching steeper until they seemed to be straight up to the very reaches of the lightning that split the black night, shattering the dark window of the sky. The stones seemed to roll toward him, and he fell to one knee. Every time he stood to run he would only get a few more steps before his foot would sink into the scattered rocks that seemed to bubble and tremble like the surface of a boiling pot of water. His ankles would disappear between stones and hold fast until he fell. The winds rushed at him from all directions, and the howling escalated at every stumbling step. It became so loud that he ran with his ears covered. Out of the wind came a howling so piercing he could hear it with his flesh. First, a tortured wail, then a high-pitched continuous yelping. Both feet lodged as if in iron boots, and he fell once more. His eyes came up to meet the imploring, glazed stare of the dog. Its tongue lolled out, its head at that unfortunate angle, it struggled to raise itself. Its breath came quick and shallow, and reeked of dark forgotten places, of caverns of fetid flesh and broken bones. Then in a voice like the whisper of sand spilling on stone, the poor creature spoke to him. Please, some water. And from his canteen Juan poured blood into the dog's parched mouth.

Juan awoke to a whimper that he realized must have been his own. In the darkness around him, five pairs of frightened eyes peered back from the edges of their beds. He checked his bedpost where he could see the hanging outline of his canteen. He unscrewed the lid and drank from it.

I AM FRIGHTENED.

Why? Of what?

The dog.

The dog is dead.

It came to me.

Last night?

He nodded.

She paused, her scowl softening as she stared at a piece of egg she prodded with a fork. Me too.

What should we do? To make it go?

I don't know. Maybe if we catch the killers. Justice will send it away. She spoke uncertainly.

On this rare occasion Juan spoke to his sister in certain disagreement. I don't think so. We are only two. They must be... dangerous.

She shrugged. Our job is dangerous.

Juan was silent.

We should go back.

Why? Juan, fearful, protested.

We can wait for them.

Do you think they will do it again?

Who knows?

Juan shuddered.

Are you frightened? she asked, but not unkindly.

Yes... But I will go.

Then it is settled.

IT WAS MONDAY and because they attended school during the day, they had to wait until the hours between dismissal and the evening meal. They shared a classroom, which also served as a cafeteria, with all forty-eight children regardless of age or comprehension level. Older students often helped the younger students, and today Patrícia's usual tutor, Felipe, watched as she struggled through her arithmetic. Felipe soon would leave the compound. After spending most of his sixteen years there, he would begin a new life in the world outside. Secretly, Patrícia would miss him.

You seem disturbed.

She kept at her problems, stiffly avoiding his gaze.

Something the matter?

It's a work matter.

He frowned. A work matt. . . Ah, he smiled, the patrol for rebels.

And bandits... or murderers.

Of course. And what have you to report?

It's secret.

Ah, yes, well... You're not in trouble, are you?

No. But...

But what?

It's Juan.

Juan is in trouble?

No. Not exactly. He's just having visitors.

Visitors?

Well, actually nightmares.

Which is it? Visitors or nightmares?

Nightmares... about visitors.

Who are these visitors?

Actually, it's just one. A dead one.

So a ghost?

. . .

Someone you know . . . knew?

Yes.

And he's scared?

Very scared.

Felipe seemed hesitant for a moment, but continued to ask questions.

Maybe he—is it a he?— She nodded. —is just coming to say goodbye. To say they—he—misses you. She seemed to ponder this. Do you remember the person's name?

No. Yes. I mean, I think he does.

Felipe nodded. Well, I'm sure there's nothing to be afraid of. Soon he will leave you and go back to where he came from.

I will tell Juan. Thank you.

WHEN THEY RETURNED to the scene of the murder, the corpse already rested in shadow. Two vultures, their beaks painted in gore, looked up from their macabre feast and eyed the intruders warily. With a wail Juan began hailing them with stones from the arroyo bed. Missing wildly, the stones skittered across the dog and past it. The birds hopped away a bit then took to the air, gradually rising into the sky to resume their patient circumspection of the fallen dog and its mourners. Juan gathered stones in a pile with nervous glances to the watchful eyes above.

We must stay until dark. Then it will be alright, Patrícia offered doubtfully.

For well over an hour Patrícia watched the dirt road for the returning bandits while Juan remained near the body wishing the flies would disappear after vainly trying to drive them off with stones. The vultures had disappeared, and Juan believed Patrícia was correct in the safety of the night at least.

AS SOON AS they came back to Juan's room, the other children told them that the director was waiting to see them. Upon entering his office, they found Felipe sitting on the old leather sofa along the wall. He smiled sheepishly at them. Patrícia and Juan stood before the desk like soldiers confronted with the commanding officer.

Children.

Buenas noches, Padre Camilo, they said in unison.

Felipe tells me you have been having strange dreams. From the past. Is that true?

Sí, Padre.

Do you remember?

The children looked at each other. Patrícia spoke for both of them.

Sí.

What do you remember?

Terrible things. Frightening. I remember death.

The old man seemed troubled by this and looked at Felipe who nodded.

I see. And do you know who this visitor is?

She shrugged.

Do you remember a name?

She shook her head. Padre Camilo, who had been leaning

forward over his desk with hands clasped before him, now
leaned back with a creaking of his chair and spread his palms
along the polished wood surface.

Patrícia. How old are you?

I am eight.

Do you remember when you came here?

The silent room turned to her, Juan included. She nodded.

And you Juan?

He seemed bewildered. I have always been here.

The man smiled gently then returned to Patrícia.

Is this visitor the same person who brought you to us?
Family perhaps?

Now the children looked at each other in perplexity.

No. Her voice was a feather brushing a smooth surface.
Juan shook his head in agreement.

The man sighed and Patrícia felt guilty as though she had
done something to displease him.

You are certain of this?

They nodded without hesitation.

I see. Well.

He then settled into his chair a bit more and began telling
them about dreams, to not be afraid, to remember they are
safe there. The mood had altered somehow, and now Padre
Camilo sought his words from a spot in the middle of his desk
rather than in the eyes of the two children. To all these things,
Patrícia and Juan listened and nodded.

HE STOOD AT the bottom of a dry well. A long tunnel reaching
up above him to the sky. The sun lit the rim above and it glowed,

a golden halo. Like hot breath, the air moved in and out around him, the throat of a giant buried deep in the earth. His tongue lay thick and swollen in his dry mouth; his clothes hung heavily on him and stuck to his sweat like a second skin. In the shadows around him, set deep into the dark cracks and crevices of the stones, a whispering. An occasional laugh, the stench of cigarettes, his beating heart reverberating off hot stone, crescendoing until he thought his eardrums might split. Above, the pale blue eye that examined him at the end of this microscope of dust and stone; around him, the murmurings, the gasps of dismal distress, of breath pulling in short and shallow like a hiss, like snakes slipping through sand on their papery bellies under a desert sky. And above again, the black motes in that eye, circling patiently, waiting for him to sleep, flying lower, closer to him. Though they were still far off he could see their eyes, crimson and flat, tearless. He felt his own breath now, rapid and coarse, his tongue draped over his teeth and lips, and the sound of his own whine now filled the hollow well. He looked down to his ribs and saw the bouquet of fouled roses that bloomed through his mange-infected skin, and water came where there should have been blood. His name, familiar in that he knew it was his, but still somehow foreign, a whisper from a tightened fist spilling sand over paper. Juan. And he stared into the light above that alone gave reprieve to his darkness.

Juan.

He reached feebly for the light, finally closing his sweating fingers around his sister's wrist. Patrícia turned off her penlight, eyeing the silent beds around them. Everyone at least pretended to sleep.

You were crying again.

I had dreams.

Did it come to you?

No. I was alone. No, I was . . . someone else. I was hurt. Like the dog.

She nodded. We have to rescue the dog.

But I thought it was dead.

Its spirit is not. Like the crosses where a person has died, we need to help its pain. It is frightened. We need to make a funeral.

Patrícia remembered. She had seen one before. A shrine for the dead. The flowers, some real and withering in the harsh light and many others plastic, faded petals with tattered edges and stems. A white cross stood among them, a statuette of the Lady of Guadalupe with beckoning hands, protecting or offering protection, in a dress the color of a washed-out sky. She remembered the steel rails behind the sorrowful shrine: rails laid out across mountains and deserts connecting even this small town to other worlds that lie beyond where the two steely lines met at each horizon. Rails that lay still in the dust, taking no notice of the pounding of diesel and the pounding of unforgiving sun. But on a bitter winter night, stealing behind departed light, these quiet rails had brought death to the town. Two teens in a battered pickup truck fell prey to the rails' deception. The boys raced to beat the cold steel with its passing breath of diesel, and the rails, victorious, had claimed their brief lives for a prize. The Lady, the white cross, the tattered arrangements of pale colors, stood testament to their passing and the families kept the shrine watered with tears.

There in town stood a sign. A sign of remembrance, of sorrow, of comfort for the spirit that fears to be forgotten. It was this that they must create for the dog.

THE BODY HAD really started to smell. Flies probed it, leaping from wound to wound in frenetic buzzings. Patrícia and Juan gathered the largest stones they could carry and stacked them near the matted and torn remains. It looked less like a dog after the buzzards had performed their ritual dissection.

Do you think it had a family?

Everybody has a family.

Not us.

Patrícia thought for a minute. We had to come from somewhere.

But now we are alone. Like the dog.

The dog is not alone. We are here, yes?

I suppose. So we are its family?

I guess so.

They arranged the stones with care, first outlining the body and then covering it from the outside in, filling in the gaps with smaller stones and handfuls of dirt and sand. The stench was nauseating and they gagged, trying to breathe through their mouths as much as possible. The rocks baked in the glaring sun, and the air blurred and shimmered above the pile as though the dog's spirit were evaporating like water into the wind. Patrícia had fashioned a cross with two pieces of mesquite bound together with twine. She had trouble keeping the crosspiece in place, and in the end it resembled an X. She wiped her dusty hands on her shirt and stood back to survey their work.

I guess that is OK.

Now what?

Now we have to say something. A prayer or something.

Juan nodded and bowed his head.

Patrícia murmured some things she heard the priest say sometimes, something about Mother Mary, something about mercy. She ended with a sidelong glance at Juan. Amen.

Amen. A whisper.

Well then, it is done. We should go now.

Patrícia turned and began walking back through the arroyo in a resigned manner, like the workers returning from the fields and the sun after a long day—tired, with heavy limbs, yet with a certain peace or serenity that comes with the illusory finality of completed work.

Juan followed along with downcast eyes but then stopped abruptly without even looking to Patrícia. He slipped the canteen from his shoulder and held it before him with both hands. Then with firm steps, he returned to the humble grave. With reverence he opened the canteen and poured it carefully over the rocks. The water disappeared quickly into thirsty cracks, and the shiny dark patches on the rocks shrunk visibly in the sun until they were gone.

Without reluctance, Juan rested the emptied canteen below the awkward cross and stood back to see. He made a nod of satisfaction and ran back to where Patrícia stood watching. Then, holding hands, they began their silent walk home.

An Inside Job

I'M A ROCK STAR. Yeah, sure. I sing and play guitar – mostly cover songs, classic rock – but I've got about a dozen original songs that are ready. Maybe ten. So I put in my time, doing the cheap gigs, taking the door, occasionally playing for exposure, but not as much anymore. Maybe for a charitable event, or that fundraiser for Wally Potter – he's got cancer, but no health insurance. Just so I can feel I am contributing in some fashion. Pay it forward, you know? Wally's a fantastic piano man, beautiful love songs, never sappy, full of jazz chords but not enough to turn off the average listener. The locals love him, but like most of us, he has no funds to protect himself.

We all load a dear fortune of gear into a limping vehicle from the last decade; health insurance doesn't fit the budget.

Me, I hit the highlights alright – Doors, Zeppelin, Floyd, the usual suspects. A Beatles tune if it rocks like "Revolution." As for my own stuff, I like to think Springsteen. Well, aiming to be in that sort of category anyway. Honest stuff, rocking like the everyman. I try to slip one original in for every dozen others. A bar over by the paper mill, Bangers, got pissed about that. It's "not what people are paying for."

So no, I haven't quit my day job. And the day job I have is about as sporadic as the rock-star gig. I work for temp agencies. Think of that restless, young and dumb phase, right after college or something, serial dating, sleeping around, never finding something just right, fear of commitment. Yet it's surprisingly steady. There are a lot of equally promiscuous companies out there, looking to throw a bit of cash at you for some work. They don't want to buy the cow, right? No benefits, no commitment. Business imitating life.

So I can pay rent, and I get to eat as a bonus. Most of it is clerical stuff. Put on a shirt with buttons and what my mother still calls "slacks" and head into a bank, law firm, or some other office scenario and catch up on all the repetitive tasks that the regular help were too unmotivated to do themselves. That or the company was too cheap to hire more staff to help them. "Filing" came up on the job description with bizarre frequency. Really? No one at the office could get this stuff done? "Wow, you work so fast," said one woman, puffy like a marshmallow, wedged into her shoes and office chair. She admired my command of the alphabet? A two-week job, the temp agency had told me. Try two *days*. Meanwhile, the ladies chatted about reality TV, good fish fries, and their yards.

After a month of these tedious "inside" jobs, I started hankering for an "outside" job. These were the physical tasks, often out in a cold warehouse or literally outside under the sun. I just wanted to use my muscles for something other than keeping my head upright for eight hours. Physical tasks have their satisfaction. I move something from here to there. A visibly verifiable task. I suppose the tottering tower of files disappearing was visually measurable, but somehow it didn't satisfy. Give me a sore muscle, make me break a sweat or form a callus. I wanted a physically demanding job. And for my sins, they gave me one.

I rolled into the job site where I was to report to Brian. It wouldn't be hard to figure out who Brian was – he was the only person there. I stepped out of my car and zigzagged around wide, murky puddles scattered throughout the potholed and frost-warped gravel parking lot. I looked down to see myself reflected black against the pale gray sky. Before me lay scattered white columns across a warehouse-sized slab of concrete – large pieces nearly as tall as a man with a diameter a bit wider than I could stretch my arms – strewn like a fallen Greek temple, some of them charred black, all of them soggy. A chemical smell lingered in the air, and some patches of standing water showed swirling rainbows. It wasn't quite ammonia, but it reminded me a bit of it, the way smelling salts call you to attention and make you want to run away.

Machinery hummed somewhere out there in the ruins. A few flatbed rail cars stood on what must have been a dead-end sidetrack right along the edge of the property. Weeds grew up through the rail ties and in the spaces between the cars and the concrete slab-temple, like the cover of Zeppelin's *Houses of the Holy* minus the naked kids crawling all over them. A pair of tracks crisscrossed that space, brown mud seeping up through bent-over field grass. A perfect sorted and stacked collection of these column chunks filled one car already, while the second car held just two.

A guy on a forklift – with a large sort of three-pronged grasping device in place of the forks, like two curling fingers and an opposable thumb – came hurtling around the corner, regulation hardhat on as if something might fall out of the sky, Major Tom coming home maybe. The forklift had chipped yellow paint and a torn sticker placed crookedly along its side that read "Safety Firs." You know, the evergreens are looking out for you. He wore jeans, a white T-shirt with half a handprint smudged across his ribs, and a packet of cigarettes rolled into a sleeve like he was one of the Jets in West Side Story. The Jets' theme drifted through my head a moment. Duh-DUN-na-na, na-nah, Duh-DUNH-na-na-na-nah-NUH.

"Are you Brian? I'm the guy from the temp agency?" I announced, up-talking as if I wasn't sure.

"I figured." He didn't get down from the forklift but unrolled his shoulder stash and pulled out a cigarette, tipping up the hard hat and leaning back like break time. "They tell you what we're doing here?"

"Not really."

"All this," he swept his arm across the view behind him, but remained looking at me, "was once a warehouse for a local paper company. The warehouse, as you can see, is gone, but the paper rolls – newspaper stuff – remain. The building burnt down around it all – they cleared out what was left of the cheap structure. Wasn't much to it to begin with. Pole barn, I guess. But the thickness of these giant toilet rolls and the abundance of fire hoses in this town saved most of the paper. Sort of. It's just a soggy mess. Anyway, someone's taking it. Your mission, if you choose to accept it, is to peel off anything that's charred – just leave that crap on the ground..." he paused and cocked his head to one side to acknowledge his correction, "the *floor*, I suppose it was... and then I come around and load what I can onto those rail cars. Pretty straightforward. And pretty pointless." He reached under the seat. "Here," he said and threw me a pair of work gloves still attached to each other by the little plastic piece from the store.

I surveyed the mess. "How long they figure that'll take?"

"Two weeks."

It's always two weeks.

"What're they going to do with all this?"

"Beats me. But they're paying. Here's your chance to change the world and make a real impact."

The paper rolls had sat out in the elements, rotting, then freezing in suspension through winter, and now rotting again as the thaw had passed. I had trouble believing this soggy paper was worth paying a couple guys to sort out. Maybe it was the insurance company. Maybe they sold it to China or something. How it all worked, I have never figured out. Accepting that I never will is one of the steps to creating a comfortably numb adulthood.

I liked being left alone with the task, no one to make small talk with, "listening" to side one of *Houses of the Holy* in my head to pass the time. The strong chemical smell became a weak background odor once I got used to it. I spent the half-hour lunch break in my car with a can of lukewarm Mountain Dew and a couple pieces of baloney tucked between two slices from a loaf of generic white bread I kept in the backseat like a Kleenex dispenser. I wasn't sure where Brian had gotten to.

After some joyless lunch-eating, I spent the rest of the day wandering among the ruins, pulling off anything charred and leaving it to rot in the puddles. The monotony of the task and the seemingly endless supply of paper rolls slowed time to a crawl, and having no one to complain to about it didn't help. At the end of the day I headed straight for my car. Brian stood in the lot leaning on the forklift, waiting for me.

"See you tomorrow," I said.

"No, you won't." He turned around and started walking away.

"Excuse me?"

"No one ever comes back," he said over his shoulder.

I LIVED IN a one-bedroom, upstairs apartment in an old house that had been divvied up into three shitty little residences. I shared rent with Roger, a freelance drummer who sat in on a few of my shows from time to time when I cobbled together a band. I had the bedroom and he had the oversized closet or storage space at the other end. The ceiling sloped sharply so he could only stand up straight at one side of his room. He spent most of his time at his girlfriend's though. Warmer in all respects. The heat from an open gas burner mounted through the wall between the kitchen and the tiny dining room was all there was for the place, and it got colder quickly the farther you ventured toward bed. We turned it off at night for fear of gassing ourselves. I had to throw plastic up over the windows and sleep with a hoodie on. It had been a tough winter and I didn't plan on being in this place for another.

That night my muscles ached, so I guess I got what I wanted from an "outside" job. The previous week had placed me with three women working in a small back office – honestly, I can't even say what it is the company did exactly – where I took a spare desk with a functioning monochrome computer on it, something straight out of a tech museum or a landfill. Filing boxes framed the monitor.

We chatted, because what else does one do in a closed space like that? I could see they weren't impressed I had dropped out of college, and they seemed to want to mother me, though they weren't even forty yet. I could have picked any one of them up at a local cougar tavern. Not literally though. They sported safe hairstyles, not pretending that their wildest times weren't behind them.

"You really ought to go back and finish. You still got time."

"I just don't see the point."

"But think of the job prospects if you don't have a degree." Martha was her name, and she added quickly, "I mean, if the music doesn't work out."

I wanted to say, "What? So I could work here like you?" But I didn't. It was true, though: they were all college graduates – in communications or business or who knows what – and slowly sinking into their chairs like goop, already unable to accomplish the menial tasks that came with the position. The college-educated position. But then here I was, expendable and working under them.

My own folks were already coming to terms with their disappointment. Dad had gone to night school to get his degree while working full-time at a hardware store. He ended up a manager at a regional department store, convinced the studies had made it happen. They still showed up for my gigs, but it seemed like a sad duty, like they were there to watch a teenage son still in tee league swinging the bat at lazy pitches from a chubby former athlete who still took five-year-olds playing baseball seriously. "Come on, guys, I wanna hear some chatter out there in the outfield!" Between songs I had at least two people clapping.

I awoke the next morning feeling like my fingernails were being extracted. Torture during the war sort of stuff. What the hell? I stared at my hands and wondered if I could even hold the guitar with them at that moment. I really didn't want to go back out into the cold, and I sure as hell didn't want to claw at soggy paper with my fingers while needle-like pains shot through them. But that last thing Brian said the day before stood like a challenge. He was right, of course: I had no intention at all in continuing with this assignment. Screw that. But then he had nailed me, like he was calling me a liar. Or a weakling. I wanted to prove him wrong, so I showed up. Rather than packing a lunch, I just grabbed a can of food from above the sink, a can opener, and a spoon. One more day, at least.

Brian's eyebrows rose as I sauntered up through the paper columns, ready for business. He stood next to the forklift, holding his cigarette in his lips as he put his gloves on, pulling short drags like he was stoking a cigar and bobbing and weaving his head a bit to keep the smoke out of his squinted eyes. We nodded to each other. I looked up and down the rows of rolls, sighed, and turned to the closest one. I tried to peel the first layer off but pulled back and clenched my fists. He saw me wince.

"What's the matter?"

"My fingers. Hurt like hell. Like someone jamming needles under the nails."

"That's bullshit. Let me get you a crowbar or something. How much they paying you? Minimum plus a dime? No one ought to be tortured for that kind of money. Needles under nails, eh? Like Japanese did to POWs."

"Yeah, I was thinking that." Or was it the Vietnamese? Or maybe just a Hollywood movie?

He came back with a bar from I don't know where. Then he climbed back on the lift and continued pulling the higher rolls down and setting them up in open spaces where I could get at them. He looked busy as hell, but it didn't seem like he was making much progress, just a lot of motion.

I went back to my car around lunchtime and saw what I had grabbed in my pre-Mountain Dew stupor that morning. Spaghetti-O's? I remembered how much I loved that fusion orange pseudo-food when I was a kid. Nothing more than some modified take on ketchup and canned pasta zeroes. I curled the opener around the lid and wiggled the last bit back and forth to take it off completely. Not as good as I remembered.

I went looking for Brian and found him parked next to the tracks, sitting upon the lift like a bored emperor surveying his ravaged empire. Nero, the morning after.

"You smoke?" At first I thought he meant cigarettes, but he didn't reach for the pack in his sleeve, and the angle of his head when he asked suggested he meant something else.

"What? Here? *Now?*"

"Hey," he shrugged, palms up, turning to and fro as if scanning the site. "Looks like I'm the boss. I promise I will look the other way." Brian had some sort of certificate for driving forklift. I guess there's a school or course for that. Same as bartenders maybe. I'm sure at some point someone had advised against substance use on this contraption with its giant claw. Pretty sure he could grab me with it like King Kong and that woman. He climbed up onto the train car and I struggled up behind him. We sat on the edge as he rolled a joint.

We passed it back and forth until he sucked at a tiny bit of extinguished paper hoping to find a spark. He took a long deep breath and exhaled, whistling through his nose. I leaned back against a roll and stared out over the empty field beyond the industrial park where a peculiar cloud on the horizon rose like smoke from a distant ship. As I sank into the paper, Brian perked right up and started talking.

He graduated from the high school on the opposite side of town, and the next day packed up his old Subaru Brat – "not quite a truck but pretending to be" – and drove a week to get to Alaska. He got a job gutting fish for "beaucoup bucks" and at some point learned to "drive fork." Then he worked a couple winters at Colorado ski resorts, where the weed was amazing, not like the "ditch shit here in the Midwest." "A couple of years ago, I moved back, because of my folks," he said, but didn't elaborate.

"We do what we have to so we can do what we want to. Of course, that shit falls apart when we end up doing nothing but what we have to." I took a second to run his statement through my head again. "See, work is like sleep. You have to do it and there's no harm or disappointment in it. But if you spend your whole life in bed?" He shrugs up his hands. "If you stop swimming and let go, the current takes you where it will."

I was still pondering the dubious claim that work was like sleep. "Is this all you do?"

He frowned. "We always ask that. What do you do? What do *you* do? What do you *do?* Like it's the first question you asked me, right?"

"Actually, I think I asked if you were Brian."

"We just drill right to it, as if what your job is defines you." He squinted at me as if letting that sink in, giving me time. "Does *this* define you?"

"Of course not. I didn't mean—"

"It sure doesn't define me. But then nothing I do does. I once wanted to be a fireman."

"Really? Like when you were a kid or something?"

"No, last summer. I thought about it. But then there's this whole long training thing, plus just getting hired is hard. Everyone wants the job. Pay is good and most of the time you aren't doing anything. Ever see those guys? Out front of the station, grilling burgers or something? They go to the grocery store with a hook and ladder."

"I guess in case they get a call when they're in there?"

"Exactly!" He points his pinched fingers at me though the tiny bit of a joint is long gone. "They are grocery shopping. Why?"

"Um, to eat?"

"I mean shouldn't someone do that for them?"

"I guess, maybe."

"So that sounds pretty sweet, right? Just paid to wait."

"Um, yeah... and fight fires? Run into burning buildings? Kind of dangerous, don't you think?"

"But mostly waiting. So then I thought, why do I want to wait to do? Wait to act. I'm on pause. I'm under glass, like, 'in case of emergency, break glass.' Which is what a fire alarm actually says, right? No, I want to *be*. I want to be *activated*, you know? A force in the universe."

"I..." I ran out of words like digging around in the bottom of an empty bag, and a wave came over me. I felt I was sinking into tingling foam, my head muffled as if I wore a motorcycle helmet. And the waves would pass and return. I wondered what ditch he got his weed out of. I watched with complete concentration as Brian lit up a cigarette.

"Did you know mouse... mice... Did you know mice can flatten their heads? Like the bones in their skulls fold or something and they can squish their own heads flat and slip right through a crack. I've seen it. It's nuts. Can you imagine? I mean, if we could do that?" He nodded his head rhythmically like a boat bobbing in a passing wake. "That'd be sweet. Like you could escape from prison and shit, head first, right through the bars." His face unfolded, a look of surprise in slow motion. "God, what's that smell?" He looked like he might spit, then exhaled a plume of smoke. "You smell that?"

"Of course."

We hopped off the car and stepped through a short obstacle course of paper rolls like pulp boulders, and there it was: a dead raccoon, like a partly deflated balloon. "Agh, that's horrible. Should we move it?" he asked, standing over it, arms akimbo.

"Are you nuts?"

"Get a shovel?"

"Smells like rotting meat in my kitchen garbage can."

"Pretty much. That's what it is. You'd start to smell like that too if you were lying out here a week or something. We're all meat."

He disappeared into the columns and came back with a big square-bladed shovel, the kind you might use to shovel shit or slop in a pig sty. I leaned far to my right trying to see or figure out where the hell he kept pulling these implements from. He slid the blade under the rumpled corpse and walked far out into the field where he gave it a good toss as if he was shoveling snow.

I watched him walk all the way back until he stood again where the raccoon had been. "'Ashes to ashes, dust to dust.' What a load of crap. I guess the stink of it doesn't go well with poetry." He had a long impossible ash of his own dangling off the cigarette clenched in his lips. It fluttered a bit as he spoke. A thin wisp of smoke curled up into his face, and he squinted one eye. He looked like Popeye or one of those old Cabbage Patch dolls that my mother kept in its original packaging hoping to somehow become rich off of them on eBay or something. We went back to our assigned tasks. Suddenly, I had a hankering for another can of cold Spaghetti O's.

That night I continued my gourmet menu with a bowl of dime-a-bag ramen while I watched a rerun of one of the *Law & Order* series. Of all the crime shows in the world, and their thousands of episodes, maybe a half dozen crimes repeated a million different ways. How many CSI versions did civilization need? Is any of it new or different? Yet I could watch them every night now in syndication, back-to-back. I set the empty bowl on the coffee table and picked up my acoustic guitar to noodle around, finding the keys to the commercial jingles and the episode soundtrack, and pushing past the lingering pain in my fingertips.

Maybe I needed a place with a bigger music scene. Like Nashville. It's not just country, you know. The people from Nashville always tell you that, and it might even be true. But if everyone and their cousin heads there to gig and busk, it's got to be even harder to stand out. Maybe there's something to being master of your own little domain. Mr. Holland and his opus at the high school. Biggish fish, little puddle.

DAY THREE, MORE of the same, though he hadn't taunted me to return. I'd come back on my own. Easily trained. Going to a job is nothing more than a habit. At lunch, I sat in my car with a peanut butter and jelly sandwich, my thumb squeezing my place in an Agatha Christie novel, splitting the old paperback's binding. Someone murdered on a Nile River cruise. It had to be much easier to off someone in Egypt. I figured bodies showed up all the time. Like the raccoon, just tucked away out of sight until the smell gave them away. Turning black and blowing up like a balloon like those road-kill deer out on the highways. I wondered if they scooped those up with something, the bodies in Egypt, I mean, or just tagged them with spray paint like the state troopers do. A death marked and recorded, now let nature take its course.

Brian shuffled over through the gravel lot, leaned against the fender eating half a dozen sticks of beef jerky before a dessert smoke.

I stayed in the car, window down. "How'd you get this gig, Brian?"

"Luck."

My mind continued to hover over bodies. "I read a novel not too long ago, set in Russia, and part of it was about snowdrops: bodies get dumped in winter so they're not found until spring. By that time, no one is looking or the killer is long gone."

"Snowdrops, eh?" He snorted.

I frowned. "Russia strikes me as a bit of a brutal place."

"Ah, yes, but at least it's honest."

"Honest?"

"No one's pretending they value a person. Not like here where you have so many people talking about Jesus and babies and veterans and whatever the hell. We drop 'em like roadkill just the same."

"A bit of a cynic, I guess."

"Realistic. Like the Russians. I don't think Russians have rosy-colored ideas about life and the world."

"They don't seem very happy, I can say that."

"They're fine. They have vodka. And we have religion."

"Opiate of the people. Sure. You're into Marx?"

"Marx used opium. He loved the stuff. Did you think he was *insulting* religion?"

I watched him with doubt and decided I probably needed to go look that up.

I told him about my music and he bobbed his head in a dude-like fashion, approvingly.

"That's cool that you have some originals."

"Yeah, but the covers get the gigs, you know? Like I'm sneaking songs in between hoping someone will notice."

"Just don't sell out, man."

"Meaning?"

"Don't do it for the money."

"I wish."

"Careful what you wish for."

"I totally wish. Making money doing what you love?"

"Covers? Pfft."

"Not just covers. But yeah, covers too. Hey, I put my twist on them. A bit."

"Imitation is flattery. But work ruins everything."

I lost where this was going, and so I stopped talking. A bird dropped its cargo right between us. Seagull, judging from the payload. "Whoa, Jesus." He leaned out to the side to look. "Near miss. You sunk my battleship."

"I have a gig Saturday at Mel's Bar. You know it?"

"Sure."

"Come on out and have a listen. No cover." I felt awkward

at his pause, as if I had made an unwanted pass at some woman at a bar.

He dabbed at a tiny bit of tobacco stuck to his bottom lip. "I just may do that."

AND SO HE DID. I opened that night for a popular local cover band playing classic rock songs. The singer was a woman, but they did mostly Zeppelin tunes, her voice magically capturing that unmistakable wail of Robert Plant.

My parents came up to congratulate me as I packed up my gear to make way for the band. Brian hung back at the bar until they left, then came forward to help carry my amp out to the backseat of my rust-colored K-car.

"Whoa, classic. 1980s?"

"'89, last year they made them."

"You should get collector's plates."

"It's only fifteen years old. Collector cars need to be twenty. What would I attach them to anyway?"

He nodded, poked the toe of his work boot against a rusty piece of the rear fender. I threw a blanket over my gear, a lame effort to discourage a window-breaking thief, and we went back in for a round of rail bourbon. I still had my bar tab covered but I bought him a drink.

"Cheers, to the future of newsprint."

He downed his in a go. We soon ran out of things to say, and he called it a night the next time I got up to pee.

THE NEXT MONDAY I arrived back at the job site under clear blue skies, the sun low but already warm on my skin.

"How are your hands?" He didn't wait for an answer but took a hit and handed me his joint. "'ere," he said with the tiny bit of air in his throat.

"Still pretty sore."

He exhaled blue. "But you can still play guitar, apparently."

I smiled.

"Never let a job get in the way of your dreams, man."

I wondered what that meant to a guy riding forklift in a shitfield of paper sludge. I spent the next hour back at it, my mind drifting to different thoughts, some of them relevant to something or anything. The pain in my hands felt distant, as if I watched it on a monitor. The weed sent ripples through my attention span, shifting waves kept lapping back to the ends of my arms, so the stabbing electricity under the nails became just a deep sensation, like warmth but not really. My fingers swelled with an energy of some kind. A comic book hero with a kind of magical touch. I walked about turning cinder black to bluish white, my superpower radiating from my hands.

Jesus, what people will do for money. And to think about all the hours I'd rehearsed and performed for no money at all. Maybe I was the fool, enduring industrial torture for cash. But sometimes our relationship with arbitrary slips of paper seems more like a cult worshipper believing reality is the illusion. The adage of "Do what you love and the money will follow" is a magnificent opiate. Works for some, but only in the dulling sense, not the cash flow.

Illusions also work. A friend I knew in high school once got high – or thought he did – on a sandwich baggie of oregano he bought from a carnie at the county fair. We got a good laugh out of it, though he still swears he caught a buzz. It did taste good on a pizza.

The forklift came barreling around the corner, and even without a certification in forklift operation, I could see the load was too high in the air. Brian came up right to the edge of the concrete, turning just in time, and then ran along that lip. I let go a breath I hadn't realized I'd been holding, thinking he had made a great save. But he wavered a bit, maybe as he reached up for that cigarette, and the tire came off the concrete and dropped an inch.

One damn inch. Within an inch of one's life, they say. And right here is what that meant. That little tilt, that small shift of weight, and the sudden deceleration of the tire hitting a softer surface dragged the whole thing down and to the left. The forklift fell forward and twisted, a gymnast putting down one hand to somersault. The paper roll slipped off and landed with a thud that was both bigger than I had ever felt but muffled by the ground. All sorts of physics that I would have failed in high school took the forklift down like a gut-shot deer, the giant claw angled into the short slope off the concrete pad, stuck in the earth, and turned the whole thing over. Brian disappeared behind it, but his painful cry was quite clear through the rattling acrobatics of the forklift.

I ran to him and found him tangled underneath, reaching into the metal for something. He didn't appear to be crushed, but he wasn't getting up either. He roared in pain, "Call 9-1-1!"

I fumbled my Nokia out of my pocket and dialed. No signal. I ran back, and he shouted in disbelief, "Where are you going?"

"Signal!" I climbed the nearest stack of paper columns, and the tiny first bar appeared. The call connected and started ringing. I looked out over the ruins again. "Nine One One, what is the exact location of your emergency?"

IT DIDN'T TAKE long for two firemen to extricate him from the forklift. He sat on the edge of the concrete, attended to by a couple of blue-gloved EMTs. Smears of blood on his pants blended in with the stains of mud and paper sludge. He stared out over the parking lot, and I wondered if he was in shock. A couple little birds swooped into the lot, hopping along, pecking randomly in the gravel as they looked for unlikely crumbs. The EMTs did what they could to protect the mangled hand and made him lie on the gurney before lifting him into the ambulance.

"Brian... you gonna be OK, man?" He looked up from his thousand-yard stare and found me. "Um, maybe see you tomorrow?" I looked at the EMT and he stared back, lips pressed in a thin line as if he wanted to shake his head No. They drove off, lights but no siren.

I stood there in the sudden stillness, alone and uncertain, as if what I'd just witnessed hadn't happened. Under a featureless gray sky, the decaying pulp, the rustling, brittle field grass from the year before, and the rusted rail cars sprawled like a dreary still life of rust belt America. I looked again at the tipped forklift and Brian's hard hat lying top up in the mud as if he'd stepped into a deep patch.

I was the whole operation, just a guy standing in the ruins of newsprint. A thousand trees or more reincarnated as white columns and now dissolving into a primordial soup. Do I keep working? I thought. What's any of this worth? The paper rolls would sit there. I looked down at my gloved hands and saw a smudge of blood already darkening and another drop on a pant leg. I thought of the mangled mess of Brian's hand and felt the dull throb in my own fingers. I listened for a moment to the low hum of town off out of sight beyond the field and the faraway line of trees. The only other sound was the crunch of gravel as I shuffled back to my car, tucking the work gloves in my back pocket.

I got in, pulled out my cell to dial the temp office, and shut the door. Looking back I saw one of my gloves darkening as it soaked up water from a puddle. "Janet? Hey. It's Travis. I'm wondering... could you hook me up with an inside job?"

Acknowledgments

IT SEEMS TO ME that with a first book one needs to thank everyone and everything that ever led up to finally putting down words to show everyone. While this is not my first book, it is my first book of fiction, something I consider to be a whole other category of challenge, risk, and reward from my guidebook work and even the travel memoir. This small collection of short stories has been a very long time coming, and it is, I hope, a tipping point.

Somewhere in boxes in my parents' basement lie the beginnings of "novels" I intended to write, dating back to middle school when I started a science fiction story *To Titan and Beyond* with a good friend, Steve Heinzen. Result: a couple installments in the school newspaper, but never finished. Likewise, my sixth-grade attempt to add another mystery in the *Alfred Hitchcock and the Three Investigators* series (What? Copyright infringement?) petered out several pages into a spiral notebook. Fast forward to high school and a few short stories I enthusiastically wrote for my English teacher, Ms. Huhn, whom I never properly appreciated until college. There, John Neary, my English professor – and soon after academic advisor and friend – poached me from the Chemistry Department. Some stories for campus publication, some creative writing classes with Kyoko Mori, and then graduation and decades of false starts, occasional completed shorts, and even a few published stories.

A novel I took a year off to try to write in Guatemala? Unfinished. NaNoWriMo 2005, a completed first draft? Forgotten on the hard drive.

Then a few years ago, I went to see Nickolas Butler read from *Shotgun Lovesongs* at Room of One's Own in Madison, Wisconsin (the first bookstore that ever let me do a reading, by the way). I liked his stuff and his honesty about his writing process (especially a candid admission about checking ESPN.com ten minutes after sitting down to write). Add one of the best pieces of advice ever, the title anecdote of Anne Lamott's book on writing, *Bird by Bird*, with its wisdom about how to tackle something that seems too big — an overwhelming number of birds to write a report about? Sit down and start writing, one bird at a time, keep going.

Plus Ann Leckie's advice during a reading about *not* trying to write for the market but for yourself, so that if you *do* get rejected, at least then you still have a finished book that you love. Finally, some kind personal words from Robert Olen Butler at a reading and via Facebook (plus his book on the process *From Where You Dream*) and Michael Perry's publishing advice years ago over a cup of coffee on State Street. You just never know how far even the smallest of kindnesses can reach.

Big thanks to Sarah Cords for more encouragement than I deserved plus publishing and story advice. To Rob Schultz, a lifelong friend and fellow book nerd, for story advice and mental support. Erica Chiarkas for years of encouragement, commentary, and emotional support. To Rob Bundy for years of embarrassing praise and the occasional stern advice. Fellow writer Andy Ravenscroft (coolest writer name ever) for commiseration, beers, and motivating mutual word-count goals. Thanks also to Paula Seymour, whose e-book success inspires me, and wisdom, knowledge, and enthusiasm guided me along. Karen Barrett-Wilt for a whole lot of reading, re-reading, re-re-reading, editing, and advice — really the lion's share of what went into this collection; definitely couldn't have finished this without her, as well as Terry Shelton, a sharp-eyed, veteran editor for a couple more final passes and a final blessing.

Finally, back to my roots: My grandmothers, Ann and Eva, and Grandpa Louie, who filled my head with family stories. My parents who surrounded me with books, took me to the library, and to bookstores when we traveled out of town. And finally, my lovely wife Preamtip Satasuk who has always supported me in this, always understood when my head was somewhere else, and always said "good job!" even when I was seemingly getting nothing done.

About the Author

Kevin Revolinski is the author of 16 books, including *60 Hikes Madison, Backroads and Byways of Wisconsin*, and *Wisconsin's Best Beer Guide*. His travel memoir *The Yogurt Man Cometh: Tales of an American Teacher in Turkey* has been translated into Korean and Turkish. His writing has appeared in a variety of publications, including *The New York Times, Chicago Tribune, Miami Herald*, and *Sydney Morning Herald*. His travels have taken him to over 75 countries, and he's lived in Guatemala, Panama, Italy, Turkey, and Thailand. Back home in Wisconsin he is an authority on camping, hiking, paddling, and craft breweries. He has been featured as a guest regularly on Wisconsin Public Radio, and once on *The Today Show*. *Stealing Away* is his first book of fiction. Find him at KevinRevolinski.com or TheMadTraveler.com.

Other Works by Kevin Revolinski

Memoir

*The Yogurt Man Cometh: Tales of an American
    Teacher in Turkey*

Travel Guides

Backroads & Byways of Wisconsin
Wisconsin's Best Beer Guide
Michigan's Best Beer Guide
Minnesota's Best Beer Guide

Outdoor Guides

60 Hikes Within 60 Miles: Madison
Best Easy Day Hikes: Grand Rapids
Best Easy Day Hikes: Milwaukee
Best Hikes Near Milwaukee
Best in Tent Camping: Wisconsin
    (with Johnny Molloy)
Best Rail Trails Wisconsin
Camping Michigan
Hiking Wisconsin
Insiders' Guide Madison
Paddling Wisconsin